CRAZY I...

"You got to stop him, ... those other two."

"I can see that," Longarm said. "Who star... ..."

"The two men, but . . ."

"Then let's just let this play out a little longer," Longarm said. "I want to watch."

"But Marshal!"

Just then, one of the men who Peacock was battling dragged out a knife and slashed at the New Yorker's throat. Longarm started to move, but before he could intercede, Peacock somehow managed to get control of the knife and without an instant's hesitation, he buried it in his attacker's chest. Tearing the knife free and spinning around, Peacock raised the bloody blade and started for his second opponent.

There was a chilling smile on his lips and that's when Longarm drew his six-gun and went into action . . .

DON'T MISS THESE
ALL-ACTION WESTERN SERIES
FROM THE BERKLEY PUBLISHING GROUP

THE GUNSMITH by J. R. Roberts
Clint Adams was a legend among lawmen, outlaws and ladies.
They called him . . . the Gunsmith.

LONGARM by Tabor Evans
The popular long-running series about Deputy U.S. Marshal
Long—his life, his loves, his fight for justice.

SLOCUM by Jake Logan
Today's longest-running action Western. John Slocum rides
a deadly trail of hot blood and cold steel.

BUSHWHACKERS by B. J. Lanagan
An action-packed series by the creators of Longarm! The
rousing adventures of the most brutal gang of cutthroats ever
assembled—Quantrill's Raiders.

DIAMONDBACK by Guy Brewer
Dex Yancey is Diamondback, a Southern gentleman turned
con man when his brother cheats him out of the family fortune. Ladies love him. Gamblers hate him. But nobody pulls
one over on Dex. . . .

WILDGUN by Jack Hanson
The blazing adventures of mountain man Will Barlow—from
the creators of Longarm!

TEXAS TRACKER by Tom Calhoun
Meet J. T. Law: the most relentless—and dangerous—
manhunter in all Texas. Where sheriffs and posses fail, he's
the best man to bring in the most vicious outlaws—for a
price.

TABOR EVANS

LONGARM

AND THE RANCHER'S DAUGHTER

JOVE BOOKS, NEW YORK

LONGARM AND THE RANCHER'S DAUGHTER

A Jove Book / published by arrangement with
the author

PRINTING HISTORY
Jove edition / February 2003

Copyright © 2003 by Penguin Putnam Inc.

Visit our website at
www.penguinputnam.com

ISBN: 0-515-13472-4

A JOVE BOOK®
Jove Books are published by The Berkley Publishing Group,
a division of Penguin Putnam Inc.,
375 Hudson Street, New York, New York 10014.
JOVE and the "J" design
are trademarks belonging to Penguin Putnam Inc.

PRINTED IN THE UNITED STATES OF AMERICA

10 9 8 7 6 5 4 3 2 1

Chapter 1

It had been a hot August in Denver and Marshal Billy Vail was feeling old and irritable as he paced back and forth in his upstairs government office. Each time he passed the window looking down on Colfax Avenue. A short distance away he could see the city's skyline dominated by the gold dome of the Colorado State Capitol Building.

Dammit, where is Custis Long?

Billy extracted his pocket watch and glared at the hands that told him it was a quarter past three. Longarm was supposed to have been here by three o'clock. It was just like his best deputy to be late when they had such an important meeting. Billy hoped that Longarm was going to be in an agreeable frame of mind because this next assignment was going to be extremely difficult.

Billy went back to his desk and plopped down in his overstuffed chair. He picked up the newspaper and once again read how President James A. Garfield was still hovering near death from an attempted assassination. The president had been grievously wounded in a Washington, D.C., railroad station by a lunatic named Charles Guiteau,

1

a disgruntled public-office seeker. While the president lay hovering near death, his vice president, Chester A. Arthur, was trying to fulfill his official duties.

Billy Vail had voted for James Garfield but he'd never liked the stuffy and inept Chester Arthur, so he said a little prayer that the critically wounded president would recover. It was a sad, sad time when the president of the United States could be gunned down. Where had his bodyguards been when the bullet was fired? Hadn't the country learned anything from the assassination of President Lincoln by John Wilkes Booth at Ford's Theater?

Too depressed by this news to read the article over completely a second time, Billy turned his attention to something more sporting. The world heavyweight bare knuckles boxing championship had been won by Paddy Ryan, who defeated the former champion, Joe Goss of England, in a brutal and bloody eighty-seven round bout near Colliers Station, West Virginia.

Good for old Paddy Ryan! Billy thought *At least something was going right in America.*

A fist hammered on his door and Billy swung away from his thoughts of bare knuckles fighting to yell, "Come in!"

Deputy Marshal Custis Long shoved his way inside, filling the doorway. He was a big man, not just tall but exceptionally wide in the shoulders and deep of chest. And Billy, despite his irritation, could not help wondering if Custis, had he possessed the inclination, was capable of whipping *both* Ryan and Goss on the same night.

The deputy marshal was that tough.

"Longarm, as usual, you're late," Billy snapped.

"Yeah, but this is my day off. Remember? So what is so important that you couldn't let me enjoy some time to myself?"

"Sit down," Billy said, mustering a nervous smile. "I'm sorry that I had you called in today. Actually, you look rather the worse for wear. Up carousing again last night?"

"I met a new lady friend," Longarm admitted, dropping into a chair and extracting a cheroot, which he jammed between his teeth. "Not that it's any of your concern."

"Did you meet her in another of our most infamous Denver watering holes?"

"If you mean a saloon," Longarm said, not bothering to light the cheroot, "then yes. But she's not what you're thinking."

"I'm not thinking anything," Billy said, feigning innocence and beginning to enjoy the conversation. "But I am wondering why you should find it necessary to meet new women. I mean, you're already up to your neck in trysts."

"In what?"

"Affairs of the heart . . . and the body," Billy explained. "How many women does one bachelor lawman need to seduce and romance?"

It was Longarm's turn to smile around his cheroot. "I always say that a man can't meet and love too many beautiful women. Wouldn't you agree?"

"If I were single and young again, I suppose I would, although there is something to be said for the blissful state of matrimony."

"Blissful?" Longarm actually chuckled. "Billy, you're the only truly happily married man that I know. All the rest are just wishing they were footloose and fancy free. That they could go out and sample the flowers that grow in Denver . . . and I'm not talking about roses."

Billy shook his head. "I'm beginning to think that you're a hopeless rake, Custis. I've tried to introduce you to respectable marriage material but, when I do, you run like a scalded cat."

3

"I'm just not the marrying kind. And besides, how would I keep a wife happy when you're always sending me out on assignments that no other deputy marshal would accept? You not only give me the worst and most dangerous jobs . . . but you also send me to places that Satan himself would avoid."

"That bad, huh?"

"Yep," Longarm said. "That bad. Anyway, I have a woman waiting this very moment. So what is so important that it couldn't hold until next Monday when I'm due back in this office?"

United States Marshal Billy Vail chose his next words very carefully, aware that Longarm was a suspicious man when it came to being assigned new investigations. "We have an . . . an unusual situation. One that requires the abilities of an unusual lawman."

"Don't bother to flatter me because that just makes me all the more suspicious," Longarm told his friend and boss. "Just lay it out straight and tell me what miserable job I've got to do next for this agency."

"Actually," Billy said, reaching for his pipe and tobacco pouch, "the job won't be all that difficult."

"Where are you sending me?"

"To Reno."

"You have a job for me in Reno?" Longarm said with disbelief. "Billy, you know that I *like* Reno. What's the catch?"

"No catch. I just remember that you had this woman in Reno. Was her name Molly?"

"No. Dolly," Longarm corrected.

"And I hear that she was not only blond and beautiful, but also rich, and that she was wild for you."

"She was a red-haired woman, and she was rich and a bit taken with me," Longarm admitted. "But she was also

4

bossy as hell and tough as a boot. She could outcuss a mule skinner and outshoot Wyatt Earp. I decided that she was a little unstable and prone to intense jealousy. The kind that could get a fella like me killed."

"I see. Is she still available?"

"I don't know," Longarm said. "And besides, I don't think her father approved of me."

"Why not?"

"Well, he owned several thousand acres of the best cattle land in that part of Nevada, and I expect that he had higher ambitions for Miss Dolly Reardon."

"Who's to say?" Billy asked. "Rancher Reardon might have changed his mind and now be willing to open his arms to a son-in-law such as yourself."

"I'm not interested in either Dolly or the cattle business," Longarm said. "So why are you sending me to Reno?"

"We've got a new man coming in, and I want you to accompany him to Reno where he'll take over as federal marshal."

"What happened to Deke Walker, the former marshal? He was a good man."

"He was gunned down last month. Didn't you know that?"

Longarm shook his head. "Deke was a friend. I'm real sorry to hear that. Did they catch the killer?"

"No," Billy said. "That will also be part of your job. You'll be helping our new man to find out who killed Walker and why."

"Is this new man I'm to accompany to Reno experienced . . . or green?"

"He's kind of experienced," Billy replied, purposefully vague.

Longarm had the distinct impression that Billy wasn't

being entirely up front about this assignment. "What does *that* mean?"

"Our new man's name is Rutherford Peacock."

Longarm waited for more information and when it was not forthcoming, he said, "And?"

"He's been a police officer in New York City for the past two years. Before that, he was a lawyer."

"A New York City lawyer and police officer!" Longarm couldn't believe what he was being told. "Come on, Billy. We both know that this doesn't make sense."

"Why not?"

"Because there's no earthly reason why a New York attorney turned policeman would come to Reno."

Billy shrugged. "Custis, I can only tell you what little I know about this new man."

Longarm withdrew the cheroot from his mouth and studied it a moment. "Billy, why would you hire a man to take over Deke's job in Reno when he has no experience as a United States marshal, much less handling our own brand of criminals? In Reno, a fella from New York City would be like a fish out of water. I'm not saying he might not be tough or smart . . . but it would take anybody a year or more to understand what is going on out West."

"Maybe he could do it in six months."

"Oh bull!" Longarm scoffed. "Nothing out here is the same as back East. You and I both know we have a whole different set of laws and values. Peacock will either get killed or be so miserable he'll quit."

"We don't have any choice in the matter," Billy said, his smile dying. "It seems that Peacock knows people in high and important government places."

Longarm leaned forward and decided to light his cheroot. This conversation was getting more troubling by the minute. "How high of places, Billy? Who does Peacock know that could get him the Reno assignment?"

"He's connected to Vice President Chester Arthur . . . who, if we are to believe the newspaper stories, is probably going to be sworn in as our president when Garfield dies. Or didn't you know about that shocking assassination business?"

"Of course I know about it." Longarm reached across Billy's desk and ran his eyes over the front page article. "It says that Garfield is slipping badly and his doctors are telling the American public to expect the worst."

"That's right. But that aside, Rutherford Peacock is closely connected to the vice president, who is already making executive changes at the highest levels."

"I'd hardly call appointing a New York City policeman an order of high business," Longarm snapped.

"Neither would I, which reinforces the fact that Peacock must be on a very close personal level with our vice president . . . soon, I fear, to become our next president."

"If young Peacock is on such good terms with a man like Chester A. Arthur," Longarm mused aloud, "why would he . . . an attorney . . . be willing to be banished to Reno?"

"That's an interesting and troubling question," Billy admitted. "And exactly the same one I've been asking myself since I got the news first thing this morning."

"Is this New York City fella already in Denver?"

"No. He's due in on this afternoon's train. I'd like you to accompany me to the station and meet him."

Longarm's eyebrows shot up. "We've *both* got to meet this guy?"

"That's right."

"And maybe they expect us to carry along a red carpet and some red roses so young Peacock will feel properly welcomed."

"Sarcasm," Billy said, wagging his index finger back and forth, "has never become you."

"Then tell me what is really going on!"

"I don't know," Billy said. "I just learned about this guy this morning. And now you know as much as I do about Rutherford Peacock."

Longarm struck a match and inhaled deeply. He blew a cloud of blue smoke toward the ceiling and shook his head. "Billy, you know what I think?"

"No."

"Without even laying eyes on the man, I think there's something fishy about Peacock that no one wants us to know. I think that he must have screwed up real bad to have been pushed out of the New York legal circles and then big city law enforcement."

"Maybe," Billy said, "but perhaps the man just wants to see the Great American West and have a new life experience. You know, Peacock might even be one of those fellas who devours dime novels and thinks there is a lot more romance out here than back East."

"Maybe," Longarm said, not sounding convinced. "But my hunch is that he's not running *to* something but instead *from* something. And I'm thinking that we need to find out a lot more about this guy before we entrust him with a federal officer's badge and office in a rough and ready town like Reno, Nevada."

"I couldn't agree more."

"So my job is to find out what he's running from and try to determine if he's going to give our agency a black eye when he pins on his badge in Reno."

"That's it in a nutshell," Billy agreed. "And also to find out who shot Marshal Deke Walker down late one evening when he was making his regular evening rounds on Virginia Street just north of the Truckee River."

"The trail will be cold by now," Longarm said.

"I know, but I have every confidence that you'll pick up the threads and bring Walker's murderer to justice. There is only one thing that I'm not sure about."

"And that is?" Longarm asked, his curiosity further piqued.

"I still wonder if you have really sworn off of Miss Dolly Reardon."

"I told you that I did. I have to admit that she was pretty exciting and fun to . . . to be around."

"I'm sure."

"But, like I said, her father is a powerful rancher and he has a much more important man in mind for his future son-in-law."

"Maybe I could write you a letter of recommendation," Billy said in jest.

"Thanks, but no thanks." Longarm drew out his own Ingersol pocket watch. "Train is arriving in less than twenty minutes. I think we'd better be moving if we want to be on hand at the station to greet this New York City misfit."

"We don't know that he's a misfit," Billy said, his expression turning serious. "For all we know, Rutherford Peacock is a good man looking for a new challenge in life. So why don't we at least give him the benefit of the doubt?"

"Okay," Longarm agreed. "But I'm almost willing to bet that he's got more skeletons in his closet than all of Denver's graveyards."

Billy said nothing as he went to grab his bowler and head for the door. He had the same feeling about this new arrival from New York City. It was a feeling that came after being a federal law officer for many years. It was a feeling that told him Rutherford Peacock would be untrustworthy and maybe much worse.

"Custis, I'm sorry that you're getting stuck with this job," Billy said as they hurried down the federal building's front steps and turned up Colfax. "But at least you're going to have the pleasure of seeing Miss Dolly again in Reno."

"She's probably already been wed and then got jealous and shot her first husband by now," Longarm told his boss. "At any rate, I have sweeter fish to fry right here in Denver. In fact, I've got one waiting for me right now."

"I'm afraid that she'll have to wait a few hours," Billy said, trying to sound sympathetic.

"Why?" Longarm demanded. "Do I also have to entertain Peacock until we pull out for Reno?"

"That's right."

Longarm stopped on the sidewalk and grabbed Billy by the arm. "Listen here," he said, voice low and menacing. "This is my day off, and I've got a very lonely woman waiting. I'm not spending my last night in Denver shuffling Peacock around like a small town promoter. So you're going to have to take him on yourself."

"Very well," Billy said, realizing that he could do no less in good conscience. "I'll take him home to my wife and family."

"Good idea. And when I come and collect him tomorrow for the ride up to Cheyenne, you can take me aside and give me your first impressions. And I expect you to be honest with me, Billy. No games and no deception. If I'm to take on this assignment, I have to figure out what caused Peacock to leave New York City after trying to be an attorney and a policeman. I *have* to know."

"I'll give you my best and most honest impression," Billy promised. "Maybe we're both wrong, and the guy is just restless. Maybe his wife or his father died and he needed to get away from the East. Longarm, it could be a very simple explanation."

"Sure."

"I mean it."

"So do I," Longarm told his boss. "I liked and respected Deke Walker and I sure can't imagine some . . . some misfit or greenhorn from the big city coming to take his place. It doesn't make sense, and the only way it can end is bad."

"That's what I love most about you, Longarm."

"What?"

"Your undying optimism."

"Go hump a hog."

They turned the corner and saw the train station at the same time they heard the locomotive's mournful whistle.

"Train is a few minutes early," Longarm commented, with a dour look on his face.

"Smile," Billy told him. "You're wearing your badge and people expect a marshal to be cheerful and polite."

"How old is this guy?"

Billy shrugged. "I have no idea. All I know is that, like you, he is also quite a man among the ladies."

"You mean he's a womanizer?"

"Is that what you are?" Billy asked, the picture of innocence.

Longarm wanted to box his boss's ears, but good sense told him that was not a wise thing to do. Besides, this job wasn't Billy Vail's doing. Hell, no. Billy took his orders just like everyone else in the government bureaucracy. Someone on high, probably in Washington, D.C., had sent the word out that Rutherford Peacock was to receive very special attention.

"I don't want you to be scowling when you meet this

guy," Billy said. "So try to be civil and not look so out of sorts."

Longarm grunted, but said nothing. He was thinking about the woman he was going to make love to in a short while and how to break the news to her that he had to leave for Reno tomorrow morning. She'd be upset, but life was always full of bad surprises.

Surprises like Rutherford Peacock, Esquire, from of all places, New York City.

Chapter 2

Longarm was very familiar with the train station because that was usually where his journeys began and ended. Most often, he rode the 107-mile Denver Pacific line up to Cheyenne where he then boarded the Union Pacific on his way westward. Tomorrow's trip with Rutherford Peacock would be no different, except that the northbound left at nine o'clock in the morning. Longarm would probably be up all this night with his new girlfriend and he'd be tired and even more out of sorts tomorrow, but he could sleep up to Cheyenne and then all the way to Laramie. By then, the sun would be low in the sky and he would be feeling rested. He just hoped that Peacock wasn't a talkative man, one of those Easterners who seemed compelled to constantly jabber.

"Wonder which one he is?" Billy Vail mused aloud as they watched the passengers disembark and begin coming down the train station platform. "I'm told that our new deputy marshal is tall with blond hair and a square jaw."

Longarm had no idea and no comment. As they stood waiting, maybe fifty people got off and collected their baggage. Several of the younger men looked like possibilities, but when Billy approached them, they all indicated otherwise.

"Could that man with the woman on his arm be Peacock?" Billy asked aloud.

"Might be, but I doubt it," Longarm said. "He looks like a banker or . . . or a lawyer."

"I wonder who that beautiful woman is?" Billy asked.

"I don't know, but I'd sure like to make her acquaintance," Longarm said, moving forward. "I'll ask."

As he walked toward the handsome couple, Longarm could see on closer inspection that the woman wasn't quite as lovely as she'd first appeared from a distance. In fact, now Longarm could see that she wore a thick layer of powder on her face to cover wrinkles and that a noticeable roll of fat pushed from under where her corset must have been drawn very tight.

"Excuse me," Longarm said, touching the brim of his hat to the lady and then facing the gentleman at her side, who was even a shade taller than himself and did have a thick, square jaw with a cleft in his chin. "Are you Deputy Marshal Rutherford Peacock?"

The man gave him a dazzling smile with the most perfect set of teeth that Longarm had ever seen. Like Longarm, he also wore a handlebar mustache, only it was blond, like his eyebrows, and his face was deeply tanned and ruggedly handsome. The man looked like he ought to be a stage idol rather than a would-be frontier marshal.

"I am indeed Marshal Peacock," he said in a deep and well modulated tone of voice as he brushed back his tailored frock coat to reveal that he was wearing two pearl-handled Colts. "And you are?"

"I'm Deputy Marshal Custis Long." He jacked his thumb back over his shoulder. "And the fella comin' up to join us is Marshal Billy Vail. We're here to see that

14

you get settled in tonight so that we can be on our way to Reno tomorrow."

"Tomorrow!" The powdered woman's hands lifted in an imploring gesture. "Oh, you can't take Ford away from me so soon! We've got some things to do and see here in Denver before we must be parted."

Longarm didn't know what to say to that, so he waited until Billy joined them and then said, "The lady doesn't want Deputy Marshal Peacock to leave on tomorrow's train. So what do you say about that, Billy?"

Billy smiled first at the woman, then at the man from New York City. "I'm afraid that you must leave tomorrow. As you're probably aware, your predecessor . . . Marshal Deke Walker . . . was murdered in Reno, and whatever clues or evidence we might have as to his killer are already growing old. So you and Custis have to leave in the morning."

"Gosh, I'm sorry. But it's been one hell of a long trip from New York City, and I'm all tuckered out. I've had some . . . well, indigestion and stomach troubles, and I should see a doctor tomorrow and get some rest. Otherwise, I could really get sick and be worthless by the time we arrive in Reno. Do you fellas know a good doctor here in Denver that you'd be willing to recommend?"

Longarm couldn't believe what he was hearing, but then, he was even more astounded to hear Billy say, "Why, yes. I go to see Dr. Holmes, and I'd be happy to take you to his office."

"Thanks, Billy."

"What about me?" the woman cried. "I ain't feeling all that good either. Do you think it was those two bottles of French wine we had on the train last night?"

Longarm could barely keep from scoffing. *Two bottles of French wine? No wonder they both had upset stomachs and the trots.* He turned to Billy wondering how his boss was going to handle this interesting predicament.

Billy took a deep breath, seemed to muster a full measure of composure and then he smiled sweetly and said, "Well, Miss, I'm sure that Dr. Holmes would be pleased to see you as well. Why don't you come along now and we'll go straight to his office."

"We have trunks to collect," Peacock said. "And we'll need them delivered to our hotel."

Trunks, Longarm thought. *This is bloody unbelievable!*

But again, Billy just gave them a sickening smile and said, "Of course you do! We'll have them delivered to the . . . the Denver Ambassador Hotel."

"Good," Peacock said.

Longarm couldn't help but turn away shaking his head. The Denver Ambassador was the fanciest hotel in town, and he'd heard that its rooms cost a fortune. *What was going on here?*

Billy hailed a horse-drawn carriage and baggage man. Soon, they were riding like royalty down the street and while Longarm sat almost stupefied with amazement, Billy, Rutherford and Miss Weaver carried on a happy conversation. The woman was clinging to Peacock like a blood-sucking leech. It made Longarm want to grab her by the front of her dress and shake her.

"Denver is . . . quaint," Peacock was saying. "Real quaint. It all looks as if it were thrown together in about a week. Nothing at all like New York City. Is that your tallest building?"

"No," Billy answered. "Our state capitol is taller."

"I'd hope so," Peacock said. "And why haven't they paved some of the side streets? All this dust and dirt. Why, it's really quite filthy here. Hot, too."

"Very hot," Miss Weaver agreed, producing a silk

handkerchief and dabbing at her face and making puddles on her powdery cheeks. "I didn't expect it to be so warm."

"It's August," Longarm said, unable to keep silent any longer. "I understand that it's not only hot in New York City at this time of year but also so humid you never stop sweating."

Both Peacock and his girlfriend glared at him as if he were out of his mind. Peacock spoke first, "The climate in New York City is quite agreeable. And I'll guarantee you won't see nearly so much horse shit littering the streets and causing a fly problem such I am seeing right now."

"Is that a fact?"

"It certainly is," Peacock said, looking quite dissatisfied with his surroundings. "I have to say that I am a bit disappointed in Denver."

"Me, too," the woman chirped. "Rutherford, perhaps I should accompany you to Reno."

"I don't think that would be such a good idea."

"Why not?"

"Well, I have to solve a murder and bring a marshal's killer to justice, so I expect I'll be very busy at first."

"But I wouldn't expect you to inconvenience yourself."

Peacock smiled but, for the first time, Longarm saw an unexpected hardness in his eyes that was also reflected in his voice. "Veronica, I said no. You can't come with me to Reno, so let's not talk about it again."

She looked away suddenly and Longarm saw that her eyes were glistening. *Well I'll be, she's actually fallen in love with this joker.*

"But," Peacock added, with emphasis better suited to a courtroom than a carriage, "I'm sure that we will find a lot of time to be together while I'm resting during the next few days."

17

"Yes," she whispered in a subdued voice, "I'm sure we will."

At least, Longarm thought, *I can spend an extra day with that new woman I met last night. At least I can take comfort in that.*

But just as Longarm was taking comfort in the fact that he would have an extra night of lovemaking, Billy looked at him and said, "It makes no sense to me that you need to stay here while Rutherford recuperates. So you can take the train out tomorrow to Reno. That way, you can get a jump on the murder investigation."

Longarm started to protest and Peacock said, "Actually, I should be there in Reno when Marshal Long arrives."

"Yes," Longarm said not bothering to hide both his disdain and his exasperation. "If you're to be the town's next federal marshal, you should be there."

"And I'd really like to be," Rutherford said, looking very disappointed, "but there isn't much point in that if I'm feeling under the weather. I've always believed that first impressions are lasting impressions. I mean, when I stepped into a courtroom, I always made sure that I looked my best. And, to be honest, I'd like it to be that way when I arrive in Reno."

"Then you aren't going with me tomorrow?" Longarm asked.

"Wish I could, but it would be foolish for the reasons I've just explained."

"Fine!" Longarm snapped. "Driver. Pull up!"

"Where are you going?" Billy demanded.

"Billy, I've got more important things to do right now," Longarm said, hopping down into the street. "Especially since I'll be leaving first thing in the morning."

"Hey, listen!" Rutherford Peacock called. "Take good

notes on whatever you find out about Marshal Walker's murder."

"Sure thing," Longarm said, so disgusted that he was barely able to speak.

"Custis!"

It was Billy, so Longarm spun around when he reached the boardwalk. "Yeah?"

"I'll see you off at the train station tomorrow morning."

"Why bother?"

"We have a few things to discuss, so get there early."

"Count on it," Longarm said, deciding right then that he wouldn't arrive until the very last minute. Billy had sold him out and he'd be damned if he'd accommodate the man any further.

Chapter 3

Longarm closed the door to his apartment with his eyes fixed on the lovely woman he had only just recently met. "So, Julia, why don't we get comfortable?"

"I am hot. I hate summer!" The room was stuffy and hot, so she started fanning herself with her hand. "Custis, I'd rather fight the snow than sweat all the time."

"Me, too," Longarm told her. "Why don't you take off something and make yourself at home."

Julia was a tall woman and from what Longarm could tell so far, one that enjoyed a fine, full figure. She had already told him that she was twenty-seven and had only lived in Denver six months. And from the way she was complaining about the hot August weather, you would have thought she hailed from Alaska instead of Kansas.

She looked around the cluttered little apartment and her brow knitted. "This place is a dump."

"It's not much," he agreed. "But then, I'm not here that often."

Julia seemed not to be listening as she walked slowly around the apartment, nose wrinkling when she smelled the week-old stack of dirty dishes. "Don't you wash *anything*?"

"I usually eat out." Longarm kicked off his boots and unbuckled his gunbelt, hanging it over the back of a chair. "Like we'll do tonight."

"Good," she said. "I can't imagine cooking in a place this downright filthy."

Longarm was beginning to get irritated, but he tried not to show it. "I'll open a window and let in some fresh air."

"Good idea! This place smells like a barn."

Longarm only had one window, and it always stuck, but he managed to get the thing wide open before turning to Julia and saying, "Are you thirsty?"

"You bet I am."

"I've got some whiskey, and there's ice in the box. I'll . . ."

She made a pouting face. "Don't you have any cool beer?"

"Afraid not."

"Water?"

"Sure."

"Then I'll have a glass of water with ice and . . . well, maybe a couple of fingers of whiskey . . . if it's good stuff."

"It is," he told her, then couldn't help but add, "I serve nothing but the best liquor."

"Yeah," she said, with a hint of sarcasm, "I can see from your place here that you'll settle for nothing but excellence."

Longarm didn't appreciate that wisecrack, but the stakes were too high to get into an argument, so he bit his tongue and held his silence. He opened his icebox and stabbed the block of ice several times and with far greater force than was required. He was beginning to think that he'd made a mistake bringing Julia to his apartment and, since it would be his last night on the town in quite some time, he sure didn't want to waste it on a complainer.

Hoping to change her sour mood, Longarm poured a liberal amount of whiskey into her glass of water. So much, in fact, that it was far more liquor than water and ice. He made his own drink quite a bit weaker.

"Here," he said, giving the woman the drink and his most winning smile, "to us!"

"To us," she repeated, raising her glass to her thick, sensuous red lips and taking a big swallow.

"Oh my gawd!" she choked, one hand flying to her throat. "That's almost straight whiskey."

He shrugged as if he hadn't known. "I hate stingy people, and I figured you for a woman who would appreciate a good drink."

Julia coughed and her eyes filled with tears. "Whew! Is yours as strong as this one?"

"Yep."

"Wow!" Julia took a deep breath, then a second, hard swallow. "Holy cow, it's so strong that I'm flushing all over and breaking out in a full body sweat."

Longarm didn't smile because, suddenly, Julia did look flushed. "Maybe you ought to come over here and sit down on the bed."

"Maybe so," she agreed.

Longarm led her to the bed and they sat there for a few minutes while Julia practiced deep breathing. He sipped at his own whiskey, then said, "Are you okay?"

"I'm fine. What kind of whiskey is this?"

"Finest you can get in Kentucky. Aged . . . oh, probably at least six months."

"Well, it's got a real kick, I can tell you that much."

"Glad you like it. Drink up." He touched his glass to her glass and added, "To us."

23

"Yeah, to us."

They both drained their glasses, and Longarm thought for a minute that Julia was going to pass out. But instead, she mopped the sweat from her face with a silk handkerchief and then she giggled. "That stuff sort of sneaks up on you, doesn't it?"

"It can," he said. "You look very uncomfortable. Why don't you take some of those clothes off?"

"You'd like that a lot, wouldn't you?" she said, her lips forming a knowing smile.

"Sure. In fact, I think I'll take off my shirt and pants. It is pretty warm in here, and there isn't much of a breeze coming through that window."

"We're on the second floor. Right?"

"That's right. Why do you ask?"

"I was just wondering if someone could peek in that window."

"Not unless they stood on a ladder or were about twelve feet tall."

Julia thought that was really funny and giggled some more. Then she burped and said, "Our glasses are empty. Do you think it would be unwise to have a little chaser?"

"I think it would be a great idea."

He jumped off the bed and made them both a second drink, but not quite as strong this time. It was Longarm's opinion, based on considerable personal research, that it was unwise to get a woman you wanted to make love to drop over drunk. A little tipsy was fine . . . but drunk was bad. When they got drunk, they fell asleep or vomited and did all kinds of unpleasant things. They often got on a crying jag or they might even turn mean and insulting. He'd known a few to get the hiccups and begin to laugh hysterically.

"Here," he said, handing Julia a second drink and then unbuttoning and removing his shirt.

"Hey," she said, eyes shining with admiration, "you're a strong-looking fella. But what are all those . . . why, they're scars! You've got scars all over your chest. Turn around. Do it slow."

"Why?"

"I want to see if you've got as many on your back."

"I don't."

"I'd like to see for myself."

When Longarm turned around, she stood up behind him and then traced a finger lightly across his back. "What's this puckered one above your right shoulder blade?"

"I was stabbed in the back by an opium-crazed Chinaman about four years ago."

"And this one under your ribs?"

"Shot from ambush in Taos, New Mexico. The doctor said if the wound had been two inches more to the center I'd be dead."

"And what about this one across your shoulders. It's long and ugly."

"I was in Abilene when a mule skinner caught me across the back with his bullwhip. It hurt worse than any bullet wound I've received."

"Turn around Marshal Long."

When he turned around, Julia reached down and placed her hand on his crotch. "Is what I'm touching also scarred?"

"No," he said. "And it's starting to feel real healthy right now."

She unbuckled his belt and then dropped his pants. "My oh my," she whispered, fingers running lightly up and down his rapidly stiffening rod. "I don't see or feel a single scar. In fact, it looks to be in perfect condition. Why, it hardly looks as if it's been used."

It was Longarm's turn to laugh out loud, and then he tossed down the rest of his drink and placed his hands on her shoulders. "It's been used a time or two."

"I'll just bet it has," she said, leaning forward and taking him into her mouth.

It felt so good and warm that Longarm closed his eyes and gave out a long, contented sigh. "This is nice."

Julia didn't reply because she *couldn't* reply. Longarm let her have her way with his manhood, and when he began to tremble with the need for release, he finally pushed her back and said, "Why don't we both get undressed and have some fun?"

Julia drained her own drink, and although she was already a little looped, it took her less than a minute to throw off her clothes and sprawl naked on his bed. She looked up and whispered, "Come take me, big boy."

Longarm was all too happy to grant that request. He mounted the tall woman and then drew up his knees so that he could lick her large nipples with his tongue. Licking and humping and bouncing and bucking, they both had a wonderful time as they began to enjoy each other's bodies.

Ten minutes later, however, they were locked in a sweaty embrace and bumping as hard as they could with Julia's long, lovely legs now wrapped around Longarm's narrow hips. Her eyes were shut tight and her lips were drawn back from her teeth.

"You ready for it?" he grunted, feeling the fire coming up like molten lava from a volcano.

"I'm ready," she panted, her own body starting to jerk uncontrollably. "Give me everything you got, lawman!"

Longarm exploded with a roar building deep in his

throat. He felt the whiskey in his gut and the seed in his belly both turn to fire, and then he was dousing out the flame, filling her own thrusting, yearning need as they emptied themselves in an orgy of pleasure.

For the next five minutes, they lay on his bed soaked with their own hot juices, like morsels of meat roasting in a hot Dutch oven. Finally, Longarm rolled over on his side and said, "You want another drink?"

"No. I'd pass out. What I need is food. Great lovemaking always makes me famished."

"Then let's get dressed and go eat."

Their clothes went on a lot slower than they'd come off and it took nearly a half hour before they were back on the street and heading for a steak house that was known to be excellent.

"It's called the Hereford," he said. "It's named after a breed of cattle whose meat is the tenderest I've ever eaten. Much more so than what you'll get from Longhorn cattle."

"I've seen it and heard of it," Julia replied. "But isn't it rather expensive?"

"Yes," he admitted. "But what the hell? I'm leaving for Reno in the morning and . . ."

"You're what?"

Too late did Longarm realize that he'd forgotten to tell Julia about his new assignment. Now, she was standing on the boardwalk with her hands on her hips looking furious. "You told me that you wouldn't have to go out for at least a week."

"I know, but my boss, Billy Vail, called me into his office and gave me the orders."

"Well, tell him we have plans. I thought we were going to hire a buggy and drive up to Central City and spend a few days in the cooler high country."

"We were," Longarm said. "In fact, I'd already reserved the horse and buggy but sometimes, things come up that are beyond anyone's control, and that's why I have to go to Reno."

Julia took his arm and squeezed it hard. "Can't you just . . . for once . . . tell your boss and the government to go to hell? Custis, we only just met but I can tell that you are tired and you need to take some time off and rest."

He thought that a bit of humor might be appropriate. "Is that what you had in mind for us? Rest?"

Julia saw the contradiction and smiled. "Actually, after the way you performed a little while ago, I probably wouldn't have given you any rest at all. But still, it would have been so nice to get to know each other up in the cool pines. I was really looking forward to going up to Central City and seeing all that mining and excitement."

"I promise that we'll go as soon as I get back."

"And how long might that be?"

"I don't know. Probably no more than two weeks. Three at the most."

She pouted and finally nodded her head. "All right. Will you write me a letter when you get to Reno?"

"What for?"

"I don't get any letters from my family in Kansas. Mother is dead and Father can't read or write. I have sisters, but they're all married, and they think I'm shameless for coming to Denver without knowing anyone. So you're all I have."

"If that's the case, then you've been hiding yourself in a closet, and I know that isn't true. I saw the way that all those men were looking at you in the saloon last night."

"Oh, there's nothing wrong with them looking. But I don't go out with men very often."

"Then why me?"

28

"Besides the obvious, which is your good looks and charm, I thought it might be fun to go out with a United States marshal. I've never been made love to by a man who wore a badge. I thought it would be exciting."

"Was it?"

"No."

He blinked.

"But next time, I want you to put that badge between our bodies when we do it."

"That's kinda crazy, Julia."

"Maybe, but I've never been pinned by a lawman, only porked."

"Porked?"

"Sure!" She slipped her hand down between them to touch a tender and still sticky spot. "You know what I mean."

"Oh, yeah!" He chuckled. "Well, whatever you like is fine with me and, if my badge would get you even more excited than you were a little while ago, why then I'd even go so far as to pin it on my butt!"

Julia gave him a very personal squeeze, and they continued down the street laughing. When they arrived at the Hereford, there was a waiting list, but Longarm flashed his badge and that gained them immediate entry into the exclusive Denver eatery.

"Nice," she said when they were seated in a dim corner. "So why did your badge get us the best table and a jump on the other customers?"

"Beats me. I guess that management just likes to keep the local authorities happy. That way, if they have trouble with someone, we arrive in a hurry and take care of the matter."

"But you're a *federal* marshal. One always on the road."

Their waiter suddenly appeared. He wore a suit and tie, white starched shirt and collar. "Good evening, Marshal and madam. What is your pleasure tonight?"

"Steak. Your best cuts."

"Rare?"

"That's how I like mine," Longarm said.

"Medium for me."

"Something to drink?"

"Whiskey?" Longarm asked.

Julia shook her head. "It couldn't begin to compare to what we've just had. How about some good French wine?"

That suited Longarm just fine, so they ordered and sat back to talk and get to know each other. But just as they were about to do that, Longarm heard a commotion in the next part of the dining room. There was loud yelling and then he heard a table and glasses crashing over.

"Marshal!" the waiter cried. "Would you please come help with this trouble?"

"Sure," Longarm said, excusing himself and hurrying after the man.

When he rounded a corner, he stopped in his tracks, for there was none other than Rutherford Peacock beating two men to a bloody pulp.

"You got to stop him, Marshal. That tall man is killing those other two."

"I can see that," Longarm said. "Who started the fight?"

"The two men did but . . ."

"Then let's just let this play out a little longer," Longarm said. "I want to watch."

"But Marshal!"

Just then, one of the men who Peacock was battling dragged out a knife and slashed at the New Yorker's throat. Longarm started to move, but before he could intercede, Peacock somehow managed to get control of the knife and without an instant's hesitation, he buried it in his attacker's chest. Tearing the knife free and spinning around, Peacock raised the bloody blade and started for his second opponent.

There was a chilling smile on his lips, and that's when Longarm drew his six-gun and went into action.

Chapter 4

"Marshal Peacock!" Longarm shouted. "Stop!"

Rutherford didn't seem to hear Longarm. His attention was fixed on the second man that he was about to stab to death, so the only thing that Longarm could do was to fire his gun into the ceiling figuring if that didn't work, he'd shoot Peacock in the leg rather than allow him to butcher his now terrified and back-pedaling opponent.

Longarm's gunshot boomed through the restaurant, sending patrons diving to the floor. "Rutherford, stop right there or I swear I'll put a hole in your damn leg."

The man from New York City finally seemed to snap out of his murderous trance. He turned and stared at Longarm for a moment, eyes crazy and unfocused. "Marshal Long?"

"That's right. Drop the knife. The fighting is over."

Peacock nodded and the bloody knife fell from his hand. His shoulders slumped and then he ran his fingers through his thick blond hair a moment before he straightened his tie. "I'm glad to see you again, Marshal."

Longarm couldn't return the sentiment. He studied the dead man whose wound was ruining the fancy carpet, then he turned to the other assailant. "What happened?"

Peacock stepped forward. "Why are you asking that man what happened? I'm the law here. These two men were drunk and they became rude and obnoxious. I asked them to leave Veronica and me alone, but they wouldn't do it. After that, things turned serious."

"I'll say they did," Longarm commented. His eyes found Veronica and he asked, "What do you say happened?"

"Those men were drunk, and they made some ugly comments about me." She came over and stood beside Peacock. "It happened just like he said. When they laid their hands on me, the fight started. Rutherford was whipping them both when one pulled a knife and he paid for his mistake with his life."

Longarm walked over to the man who had barely gotten away with his life. "You drunk?"

"We had a few drinks," the man said. He was large and strong looking, but his nose had been broken and the lower part of his face was coated with gore. "We was just funnin' 'em some when that son of a bitch went crazy. Next thing I know, we're trying to defend ourselves."

"Right," Longarm said sarcastically. "Two against one, and it was Marshal Peacock's fault that this trouble began and your friend got killed."

"It wouldn't have gone so far if he hadn't gone crazy," the man said sullenly.

Longarm shook his head. "You're under arrest. I'll take you over to the sheriff's office where you'll be put in jail and held until you see a judge."

"Why me?" the man with the broken nose shouted. "All I did was give the lady a couple of winks and a compliment or two. That tall man you call Peacock, he's the one

34

that went crazy and killed my friend. He's the one that ought to be going to jail instead of me."

"I don't see it that way," Longarm told the man. "So grab your hat and let's go."

"Yeah, right," the man sneered. "You badge totin' bastards always stick together."

"Another comment like that," Longarm said softly, "and I'll pick up that knife and cut out your lying tongue."

Just then, Julia appeared. She took in the situation and joined Longarm. "Do you have to leave now?"

"Yes, but don't worry. The jail is just a block up the street. I'll hand this man over to the local officials to be locked up and then I'll be right back. Probably even before our steaks arrive."

Peacock stepped forward. "I'm really sorry to have interrupted your dinner. I'm the one that should take this man to jail."

"Oh no!" the prisoner cried. "I'm not going off alone with that murdering bastard! He'd probably kill me and claim it was self-defense." He turned to Longarm, eyes now pleading. "Please. You take me to jail. I promise I won't cause you any more trouble. But don't turn me over to Peacock. I'm begging you!"

Longarm could see that the man was genuinely terrified. "All right. What's your name?"

"Jim. Jim Colburn. My friend's name was Pete. Pete Kendall."

"Okay, Jim. Let's go to jail."

"What about me?" Julia asked.

"She can join us while you're gone," Peacock offered. "I'll buy us a bottle of wine and we'll all settle down and try to forget this disagreeable business."

"*Disagreeable business*?" Longarm asked, looking

down at the dead man on the floor. "Is that what you call a man getting stabbed to death?"

Instead of a reply, Marshal Peacock turned to the head waiter and shouted, "Get that body out of here and clean up the mess. What kind of a restaurant is this?"

"Julia, this won't take long," Custis promised. "I'll be back in less than half an hour."

"Just hurry," she said as the head waiter ordered his assistants into action. By the time that Longarm had his prisoner outside, the late Pete Kendall's body had already been dragged through the kitchen and laid to wait for a mortician in the back alley.

Thanks to a new man at the sheriff's office, it took Custis much longer to process the prisoner than expected.

"I just need to get the details," the local lawman kept repeating as he nervously searched for a pad and pencil. "I just need to have everything down on paper so that tomorrow, when the sheriff arrives, I've got it all recorded. He wants written reports on even small crimes, and I'd say this stabbing was far more important."

"I agree. But I've told you everything there is to say. This man and his friend, a fella named Pete Kendall, were drunk and they began to harass United States Deputy Marshal Rutherford Peacock."

"How do you spell Rutherford?"

"Hell, I don't know, and I don't care!" Longarm exploded. "I'll have Peacock come by in the morning and make a full report."

"Peacock," the new lawman said, concentrating hard. "I've heard of Wild Bill Hickock, but never a Peacock."

"I don't care what you've heard," Longarm snapped. "I've got a woman and a steak both waiting at the Hereford, and I'm not going to stand here tonight and answer a bunch of fool questions."

"Look. I'm really sorry to hold you up," the deputy said, looking apologetic as he continued to claw through the desks seeking writing materials. "But the last time I had someone bring in a killer I didn't get enough information and . . ."

"I didn't kill anybody!" Jim Colburn shouted from his jail cell. "Marshal Long, you got to stay here and make sure that this idiot gets the story straight. Otherwise, I could *hang*. And I sure don't want everyone to hear just Marshal Peacock's version of what happened tonight. He's the one that turned what was just a little funnin' into a stabbing! He's the one that should be here instead of me."

Longarm shook his head with exasperation. The new deputy looked confused and rattled, and there was just no way that he could leave the man without helping him find the damned paper and pencil so he could get his facts straight.

"All right," Longarm said wearily. "Let's find something to write on, and I'll put it down on paper so there's no more confusion as to what happened at the Hereford."

"Oh thank you!" the deputy breathed. "I sure would appreciate that. And would you sign your name so that if there are any more questions, we can get ahold of you tomorrow?"

"I'm heading out to Reno first thing in the morning," Longarm said. "But Marshal Rutherford Peacock will be staying a few days, and I know he'll be more than happy to come by tomorrow and answer any questions your boss might have as to the circumstances of tonight's fatal stabbing."

"Good! That's great. But I sure would like to know how to spell his name."

Longarm couldn't believe the denseness of this deputy. "All right. We'll find a paper and pencil, and I'll spell his name for you and also that of our boss, Marshal Billy Vail, who is in the federal building."

"The federal building over on Colfax?"

"That's the one."

The deputy finally located a pencil and paper. "Okay," he said, thrusting the materials at Longarm. "Just write down exactly how it all happened."

Muttering an oath under his breath, Longarm took a chair and began a written report. It would take him maybe a half hour to put down just what he had seen, but he supposed that this was necessary because he was leaving on tomorrow's train. But dammit, Julia would be steamed and his steak would be getting cold.

When Longarm finally did get back to the Hereford, he discovered that Peacock, Veronica and Julia had all been relocated to a different room. Not only that, but they were working on a second bottle of wine and acted as if they were having a grand old time.

"Welcome back!" Peacock called, his voice a little slurred from drinking. "Your steak came and went but we can sure as hell order another."

"Thanks a lot," Longarm said, noticing how the man had his arm casually draped not only around Veronica's shoulders, but Julia's as well.

"When you finish your steak, we're going to do this town," Julia told him. "Rutherford wants us to show him all the most fun places to eat and drink. We're going to have a drink in every water hole in Denver before the night is over."

"That's right, old man! And I'm buying."

Longarm didn't care who was buying because he had other plans. Like going to bed early with Julia and enjoying another fantastic bout of lovemaking before sleep. He was in no mood for hitting all of Denver's best saloons. It wasn't that he didn't like to have as much fun as the next person, but to celebrate after the stabbing death of a man—even one that might have had it coming—seemed callous and wrong.

"Peacock," he said, looking at the handsome Easterner, "in the morning, you're going to need to go into the local sheriff's office and write up a report on what happened here tonight."

He looked surprised and then annoyed. "Why would I have to do that? Didn't you tell them the circumstances?"

"Yes, but since you're the one that stabbed Kendall to death, both the sheriff and the judge are going to want a full written report. And I expect the judge might even want you to be on hand when Jim Colburn goes into court."

"What a waste of my time! For crying out loud, Custis, there are a dozen people here that saw exactly what happened in this restaurant. They'll back me up when I say I was forced to defend the honor of Miss Weaver."

"I'm curious about something," Longarm said. "Did you identify yourself as a United States marshal to those two drunks?"

The question caught Peacock off guard, and he stammered for a moment, then took another drink of wine before looking up and firing back his own question. "And what difference would that have made given the circumstances? I mean, if I *weren't* a sworn officer of the law, would I have had any choice but to take the same action to protect Miss Weaver's honor?"

Longarm shrugged his broad shoulders. "Maybe. Maybe not. But I think it might have changed the course of events."

"Meaning that those two thugs would have backed away?"

"That's right."

"But then they'd probably have accosted and insulted some other lady and perhaps her escort wouldn't have been able to defend her honor."

"What's your point?" Longarm asked bluntly.

"My point, Marshal Long, is that I was challenged, and I responded the way a man ought to respond when a woman is insulted and laid a hand upon. What happened to the one who pulled the knife on me is exactly what should have happened. He tried to kill me, and I defended myself. It was an act of self-defense, pure and simple."

"I expect you're right and that the judge will see it the same way. But what about the second man that you were about to kill? That wouldn't have been self-defense."

"I . . . I wouldn't have killed him."

Longarm's eyebrows raised. "Oh? It sure looked to me like that was what you had in mind."

"You have no idea what I had in mind, Marshal Long. And frankly, I am both baffled and disappointed that I am having to defend my intentions. I thought we were going to be working together. And here you are, trying to put me into a position where I have to defend myself a second time this evening, only now it's with words."

Longarm came to his feet for he'd suddenly lost his appetite. "You should have shown that pair your badge and . . . if you thought they were dangerous, drawn your gun and placed them both under arrest. Getting into a fight and then burying a knife in a man's chest isn't the way it's done by a lawman."

Rutherford Peacock came to his own feet and his eyes were hard and bloodshot. And although his words were slightly slurred, there was no mistaking the fury that was rising up in his throat. "I'm not going to listen to any more of your crap. I did what I had to do, and I'm damned sorry that you aren't man enough to understand that. But . . ."

Longarm started to grab Peacock by the throat but Julia jumped between them. "Stop it! Both of you. What's the matter here? We were having fun, and we've got the whole night still ahead of us."

"Not me," Longarm grated. "If you want to go on a binge and celebrate tonight, then you'll do it with *them*. I'm going back to my apartment and calling this party quits."

Julia looked at Rutherford who had a cocky sneer on his lips and then back at Longarm and said, "I think you're being unreasonable. You're also jealous of Rutherford because he whipped both those two men while you probably couldn't have."

"That ties it," Longarm growled. "I'm leaving."

"You were leaving anyway the first thing tomorrow morning!" Julia yelled as Longarm headed for the front door. "So what have I lost?"

Longarm didn't bother to reply, and he knew that he wasn't going to go back directly to his apartment. He needed some fresh air . . . lots of it. And he needed to try and sort out what kind of a man he was dealing with in newly appointed Marshal Rutherford Peacock.

His first impression had been that the man from New York City was a dandy. Someone who stood no chance in a town as tough as Reno, where he was supposed to become the law. But after seeing Peacock use his fists on Colburn and Kendall, and then the way he had somehow managed to tear the knife free and bury it in his opponent's chest, Longarm knew that he had vastly underrated the new marshal.

"He's crazy and as cunning and deadly as a puma," Longarm muttered to himself as he followed Cherry Creek, lost in his dark ruminations. "That man is not at all what he seems, and he's going to either get himself killed in Reno . . . or get me killed. Maybe get us *both* killed, not to mention a whole bunch of other people who might cross his path or in any way give him an insult."

Longarm walked for almost an hour. Then, realizing he had still not had his supper, he found an all night eatery near the U.S. Mint on Cherokee. The food was plain but plentiful, greasy but good. Longarm found he had regained his appetite but he still had grave doubts about the soon-to-become new marshal of Reno, Nevada.

Chapter 5

Longarm hadn't slept at all well that last night in his apartment. He'd tossed and turned and he woke up feeling tired and out of sorts. His train was due to leave at nine o'clock, but he had decided that he really ought to be at the station early, so he could tell Billy Vail about Rutherford Peacock stabbing a man to death at the Hereford. And he'd tell his boss that the killing had not been necessary and, if Longarm had not interfered, there would have been a *second* stabbing death. He would advise Billy to find some way to strip Peacock of his badge and his authority. They sure didn't need a crazy, murdering marshal on the federal payroll.

When Longarm arrived at the train station, he was surprised and not one bit pleased to see not only Billy, but also Rutherford Peacock.

"Good morning," Peacock said as cheerily as if they were old friends having a long awaited reunion.

"What are you doing here?" Longarm demanded.

Peacock sighed. "I wanted to apologize for last night."

"You mean for stabbing a man to death when you should have arrested him?"

"That's not true!" Peacock's smile was slipping badly. "Look. I did what I had to do. You saw that man lunge at me with the knife. I was just lucky to wrestle it from his grasp."

"Maybe so," Longarm replied. "And then you should have drawn your gun and ordered him to raise his hands or you'd crack him across the skull. But you didn't need to turn the knife around and bury it in his heart."

Peacock shook his head. "I was hoping that my apology would get things right between us, but it seems that you're bound and determined that we should keep rubbing each other the wrong way. Marshal Vail, I told you that Long wouldn't listen to me."

Billy glanced at his watch, then to the train which was about to depart. "Rutherford, why don't you get on board while I have a word with Marshal Long."

Longarm was furious. "Is he going with me to Reno?"

"That's right," Billy said. "He's going to be the federal marshal there. Remember?"

Longarm grabbed his boss and dragged him away so they could talk in private. "Listen, Billy. I saw exactly what happened last night in that restaurant, and I tell you that Peacock is a crazy son of a bitch. I saw the look in his eyes."

"Oh come on!" Billy exclaimed. "Let's not get carried away here. I had a nice talk with Marshal Peacock this morning, and his version of the stabbing makes sense to me."

"He would have killed the second man," Longarm stated.

Billy frowned. "Custis, how many men have you had to kill in order to save your life or that of someone else?"

"What in blue blazes has that got to do with Peacock being some kind of maniac?"

"Self-defense is a justifiable response for anyone," Billy answered. "There were two of them at that restaurant against Peacock. Up until I heard his story, I was, quite honestly, worried that the man would be easy prey in Reno. It would seem to me that I badly underestimated him and that he *is* man enough to handle the job."

"No," Longarm argued, "you're wrong. As sure as we are standing here on this train platform, Peacock is going to give our agency a black eye, and he'll probably get not only himself killed, but me as well."

"You're overstating the case," Billy said. "Why don't you try to get along with our new marshal and cooperate with him in Reno. I think you just got off on the wrong foot. Hell, Custis, you might even be friends if you give the man a chance."

Longarm glanced over at Peacock. The fact that Veronica *and* Julia had come to say good-bye to the Easterner did nothing to improve his temper.

Billy shook his head. "Marshal Peacock is a man who sure attracts the women. Two of them came to give him a send-off! What happened to your woman, Longarm?"

"You're looking at her."

"Which one?"

"Julia is the taller of the pair."

Billy frowned with confusion. "If that's the case, then why is she hugging Peacock?"

"We had a little disagreement last evening after the stabbing. It's not worth retelling."

"Well," Billy decided. "When it comes to attracting the ladies, it looks like you might have finally met your match."

"They're not ladies, and I haven't met my match in anything that has to do with that crazy Easterner."

"Custis," Billy said, leaning closer and trying to talk

over the piercing blast of the train's whistle. "I explained to you that Peacock has tremendous political influence. We don't know how much, but I can tell you that he could ruin both our careers if he chose to get nasty. He's not a man that you want as your enemy."

"So you're just turning your face to what he did last night, and you expect me to do the same?"

"Just try to cooperate with him. Peacock didn't know Deke Walker, but when I told him how the man was shot in the back from ambush, I could tell that he's just as anxious to find the killer as we are."

"Oh?"

"That's right. And I don't have to tell you that Reno is a rough town, and there's some big money that flows off the mountains from Virginia City and Gold Hill. Money that has influenced Nevada politics and perverted justice. So I think you're going to need Peacock's help in order to find out who killed our friend, Deke Walker. It could be that he was murdered by someone he'd arrested or sent to prison. But it could also be that Marshal Walker was eliminated by powerful men in that city."

"We'll see," Longarm told his friend as he started to turn and board the train. "But I'll tell you one thing for sure."

"What's that?"

"If Peacock kills another man that could be arrested, then I'll tear that tin star off his chest and cram it down his throat."

Billy shook his head. "By all rights I should order you to stay here in Denver. I just ought to send another man in your place."

"That's fine with me. But I'll tell you something, Billy. We've got a sidewinder here and before the dust clears, a lot more people are going to die."

46

Longarm didn't wait for a response. He just turned on his heel and walked toward the train.

"Custis!" It was Julia and she was hurrying over to intercept him before he could board. "Custis. Wait a minute."

He paused and then turned. "What do you want?"

"I want you to take care of yourself in Reno. And to take care of Rutherford."

Longarm was so surprised and disgusted, he boarded the train without bothering to reply.

Longarm didn't see Peacock until they changed trains that afternoon in Cheyenne and headed west over the Laramie Mountains. He was dozing in his seat when the former lawyer and New York policeman entered his coach.

"Marshal Long, we need to talk in private."

Longarm's hat was pulled down low over his eyes and he started into wakefulness. Gazing up at the tall, handsome man, he asked, "I don't think you and I have anything to say to each other."

"I disagree. And I insist. Why don't I buy you a drink in the first-class coach where I have a special compartment. We won't have to worry about being overheard."

Longarm was traveling in third class and that rankled him. But instead of telling Peacock to go to hell, he decided to hear what he had to say. "All right."

"Good."

When they got to Peacock's first-class compartment, Longarm was ushered inside and found that it was quite luxurious with a soft velvet covered chair, a bed, sink and even a commode.

"Have a seat in that chair," the man offered. "I'll pour us a couple of glasses of brandy I bought in the dining car."

Longarm said nothing, but accepted a crystal tumbler generously filled. Peacock said down across from him on the folded up bunk and said, "Let's have a toast."

"To what?"

"To a new beginning between us. And to finding out who murdered Marshal Deke Walker."

Because the second part of the toast was acceptable, Longarm raised his glass and took a sip. Smacking his lips, he said, "This is excellent brandy."

"It's the best I could get under the circumstances," Peacock told him. "But it would be considered inferior if we were drinking in a New York City saloon."

Longarm eased back in the chair, unbuttoning his coat and loosening his tie. "So why didn't you stay in New York?"

"I have my reasons. Mainly, though, I just needed a change of scenery."

"What about your law profession? You must have made a whole lot more money doing legal work than you'll ever earn as a deputy marshal on the wild Western frontier."

"Of course. Probably ten times more. But when is enough enough?"

"I'll never know the answer to that one," Longarm admitted. "Are you rich?"

"As a matter of fact, I am."

Longarm studied the man across the short distance that separated them. "I just don't get it," he finally confessed. "What really makes you tick?"

Peacock allowed himself a tight smile showing those perfect and brilliant white teeth.

No wonder the women make fools of themselves over Rutherford Peacock, Longarm thought. *He's not only handsome, but rich and debonair.*

"My father was a New York policeman. One of the best

sergeants that ever wore the uniform. That's why I followed in his footsteps even though I didn't think it was my calling. But I excelled, and it didn't take me long to start climbing the ladder with promotions."

"So what happened to derail your career?"

"What makes you think it was derailed?" Peacock asked. "Is it inconceivable to you that maybe I just got tired of seeing criminals released because of slick lawyers, under-the-table payoffs and corrupt politics?"

When Longarm didn't answer, Peacock continued. "I saw outrages that you wouldn't believe could happen in America. New York is riddled with crime on every level from the very rich to the very, very poor and oppressed."

"I imagine all big cities are a quagmire of graft and corruption," Longarm said. "But what I *can't* imagine is you setting out on a crusade to make things right."

"Why not?"

Longarm could have said something hard but instead, he replied, "It doesn't fit your personality."

"What makes you think you know my *personality*?"

"Mind if I smoke a cigar?"

"No."

"Care for one?"

"No, thanks."

Longarm was glad. He had forgotten to buy enough of his favorites for this trip. They were called "Cubans" and maybe they really were from Cuba but, if so, they were grown in a peasant's weed and manure field. It took some real getting used to in order to appreciate their powerful, almost mind-reeling qualities.

He lit one of his cigars and frowned. "Marshal Peacock, how old are you?"

"Why do you ask?"

"Are you even twenty-five?"

"Yes. I'm pushing thirty," Peacock said. "What's the point? Are you thinking that being a year or two older makes you far wiser? Because if that's what you're about to tell me, then I'll tell you that I've probably seen more trouble and danger in my life than you have in yours."

"But you're a rich boy. I can't quite imagine you've ever had to deal with that kind of thing."

"Oh, but you're wrong." Peacock's eyes shuttered. "That cigar stinks. I'd either better have one or I'm going to have to toss yours out the window."

"You could try," Longarm said, offering the man a cigar because he was drinking Peacock's excellent brandy.

"Like I said," Peacock began, "my father was a decorated policeman. And when I was just a kid, all the city toughs would try to get back at him through me. I had to learn fast how to defend myself against bullies. My father had been a bare knuckles fighter and he taught me well. By the time I was thirteen years old and big for my age, I was whipping grown men. By the time I was twenty, I was earning most of my money fighting in the ring. I could have been a world champion but I chose to enforce the law."

"How noble of you," Longarm said cryptically. "Did your father also tell you to kill a man when it was in your power to merely knock him unconscious?"

"My father," Peacock said, with an edge to his voice as he lit the cigar, "told me that the first thing you do in any fight is to win. He told me that there is no such thing as a 'fair' fight. Would you disagree?"

"Not entirely. But you were whipping both those drunks at the Hereford and enjoying yourself."

"Nonsense!"

"It's true. There was a smile on your face and a look

50

in your eye that told me you were having one hell of a lot of fun."

Peacock frowned. "I do enjoy administering a physical lesson in manners. They were drunks and bullies and expected me to cower and plead. I suspect that the one who survived will never try to humiliate anyone again or insult a woman."

"Probably not."

"But what you really need to know," Peacock said, "is that I am sorry that I killed that man. He had a hideout derringer that he was reaching for when I took his knife away. Did you notice?"

"No."

"It was hidden in his left coat pocket. His friend, the one that you feel so good about having saved, was also about to reach for a knife in his boot top."

"Not true," Longarm said. "I searched him for weapons when I got him to the jail and he was . . ."

"What?"

Longarm could have sworn out loud. "I was in a rush and didn't think to look in his boot top."

"If you had, you would have found the knife. I saw it when he fell back and his pants' leg came up over his boot top. Jim Colburn made sure that it was covered when you stepped into the picture, but I assure you that he would have tried to use it on me if you hadn't interfered."

Longarm had to admit that he'd been lax in not checking Colburn's boots and that made him angry at himself. "I might have made a mistake, but I would not have had to kill anyone like you did."

"I had a woman to think of in addition to my own life."

"You were in a crowded restaurant."

"So what? Custis, they were both drunk and looking for a fight. But why are we going around and around about this? Why can't we patch things up and see if we can do a good job when we get to Reno? Doesn't that seem like the right and smart thing to do?"

"Sure it does," Longarm answered. "However, to be blunt, I don't trust you."

"Maybe I can make you change your own mind."

"Maybe," Longarm said. "But you're going to have your hands full just keeping law and order in Reno. Why don't you let me do all the investigation of Marshal Walker's murder? I knew the man, and you didn't, so I can work some angles that you wouldn't even be aware of."

"Such as?"

"Such as Walker had a lot of old enemies on the Comstock Lode."

"Who, exactly?"

"I can't say."

Peacock wasn't pleased. "Can't or won't?"

"Take your pick," Longarm said flatly. "But I mean to cut my own bait and set my own hook."

"I think that would be unwise," Peacock told him. "I think that you need to cooperate with me just in case you meet the same tragic fate as Marshal Walker. In that case, I could find and bring to justice whoever killed you both."

"If I agree to cooperate with you," Longarm said. "What promises do I get in return?"

"I agree to consult you before I kill anyone."

Longarm wasn't sure that he'd heard correctly. "Would you repeat that?"

"Other than defending myself against a sudden and unprovoked attack, I'll talk things over with you before I kill anyone. And I'll try to arrest people and go by the book."

"Great." Longarm drained his glass. "Anything else?"

"Yes," Peacock said. "I didn't take your woman to bed."

"She wasn't *my woman*," Longarm told the Easterner. "And even if she were, I'd have said good riddance."

"Yeah. I was glad to get rid of Veronica. I love women, but I'm sure not ready to settle into harness. It's a lot more fun to sample everything that grows in the garden."

"That it is," Longarm said, still trying to figure the man out.

"You and Marshal Vail are pretty close friends."

It wasn't a question, and Longarm didn't bother to give it a reply.

"He told me that you were his best and most trusted deputy marshal," Peacock continued. "Billy Vail told me that you were the best in the business."

"It might not be evident from his looks, but Billy was also a damned good deputy marshal in his younger days. But he fell in love, got married, had a couple of kids and . . ."

"Got fat and soft before his time," Peacock interrupted. "That's another reason why I have no desire to settle into a rut. I want to be a Western town marshal. I like challenges, and when I get Reno straightened out, then I'm going to be wanting to move along and find another town to tame."

"Doesn't surprise me," Longarm said. "Your past history tells me that you are a restless but ambitious man. You ever think about going into politics?"

He smiled. "Why do you ask?"

"You seem like the kind of man that would want that kind of power."

Peacock might have gotten offended, but instead he chuckled. "I once asked my father the same thing. And you know what he told me?"

"Nope."

"He said that politicians were just high-priced whores. Said he'd never met one that wasn't influenced by personal gain."

"Speaking of which . . . how did you become rich if you had such a poor and tough childhood as the son of an honest city policeman."

"I got rich when I was an attorney. I was fortunate enough to graduate from a prestigious school of law and meet the right kind of people. One of them was nearly as rich as an Egyptian king. He had no children . . . just a scheming wife who was thirty years younger than himself. He suspected that she had lovers and was plotting to stage his demise and then inherit his fortune."

"I'm beginning to get the picture."

"Yes," Peacock said, "I'm sure you are. At any rate, I trapped the wife, got the hard evidence of her many trysts and lovers. Then, when I presented it to my old friend, he set about getting a lawful divorce. Given our evidence, the young woman had little choice but to accept our terms and go her own way. She still made thousands, but not the millions she would have inherited."

"I see," Longarm mused aloud. "And in appreciation for both your investigative work and your legal expertise, the old gentlemen paid you handsomely."

"Better than that," Peacock said. "He left me most of his fortune."

Longarm digested this news for a few moments, then said, "Tell me one more thing."

"Sure. What is it?"

"Did you bed the old gentleman's young wife?"

Peacock grinned.

"I thought so," Longarm said. "And did you tell the old

gentleman that you'd had his young and, no doubt, beautiful wife?"

Peacock's grin faded. "I didn't think it was relevant."

"No," Longarm said, "I wouldn't think you would. How much did you inherit?"

"Enough to do whatever I want with the rest of my life."

"And so you chose to come out West and be a town marshal."

"That's right. When I was a boy I saw Buffalo Bill Cody's Wild West Show. Saw all those Indians, buffalo and cowboys. Saw old Wild Bill shoot white doves out of the sky and saw Annie Oakley. Saw them right there in New York City, and I swore that someday . . . I'd go West and make my own legend."

"And that someday is about to start."

"Yes, it is," Peacock said. "And I'd like you to be a part of it in whatever way you choose. I have the means, the guts and the brains to go a long, long way. And based on what Marshal Vail has told me, you could be a real big help."

"I already have a job," Longarm said. "And so, for that matter, do you."

"Of course. But there is nothing that says we have to be lawmen forever. Let's do our job in Reno. Let's do it fast and well and with some flair. I'll make sure we get the right . . . attention. I'll make sure that your name is in the national press right alongside my own. We'll make a hell of a combination. We'll be sensational."

Longarm clucked his tongue in admiration. "You have it all figured out."

"I plan ahead my every move, Marshal. I've found that a man without a plan is like a ship without a rudder or navigational course. But, if you think otherwise and don't wish to join me . . . then I'll understand."

"Is that a fact?"

"Yes," Peacock said, his voice turning serious. "I'll do my job and you'll do yours, and then you'll go back to Denver and leave me alone."

"To what purpose?" Longarm asked. "You see, Billy and I . . . along with a lot of other lawmen, take our roles very seriously. None of us would be willing to let someone with your kind of ambition, money and connections dirty our profession."

"Oh, I'd never do that! My father is dead now, but he felt exactly the same way that you do. And I swear on his grave that I would never besmirch the profession of upholding the law."

For some reason, Longarm believed the man. Really. "All right," he said, "how about a refill of brandy, and isn't it about time for dinner?"

"It is," Peacock said. "So are we going to work together, or are we not?"

"We are," Longarm said. "Just as long as you remember your father and don't cross the line and become the law unto your own self."

"Never!"

"Then let's have another glass of that brandy and go eat."

"I'm buying."

"All right," Longarm said. "As long as you understand that you're buying a meal and not a man."

Chapter 6

"Elko, Nevada," the conductor called. "Elko, coming up in thirty minutes!"

Longarm had been sound asleep, but now he roused himself into wakefulness. The trip across Wyoming and then Utah had been uneventful. They'd crossed the salt and alkali flats of the Great Salt Lake desert country and now they were in northeastern Nevada. It was a dry country filled with low, sun-blasted mountains and oceans of sage. There wasn't a lot to look at except the distant, snow-capped Ruby Mountains where Longarm had trailed a notorious murderer and horse thief for two weeks and nearly gotten himself bushwhacked. He'd killed the outlaw and had to walk thirty miles without water through the dangerous Paiute Indian country. It had been one of his hardest jobs and had taken him weeks to recover physically.

"Does all of Nevada look like this?" Peacock asked, settling in next to Longarm without invitation. "I sure expected handsomer country."

"This *is* the handsome part," Longarm replied. "From here on to Reno is nothing but high desert country."

"Someone told me that Reno was green country."

"It is. The Truckee River comes down from the Sierras and flows through the middle of town. But it drains out into the Humboldt Basin and just disappears in the sage and the sand."

"I see. What is the High Sierra country like?"

"It's nice up there," Longarm told the man. "Lake Tahoe is only a day's ride up the mountain. I've never seen a more beautiful alpine lake. In the summer, when the temperature around Reno is a hundred, you can take the train up to Lake Tahoe and dive into that lake and think you're in Alaska. The water is as cold as ice, but it sure feels good. They do a lot of logging up on Lake Tahoe."

"And prospecting?"

Longarm shrugged. "The forty-niners panned and mined about all the gold out of the Sierras. On the western slopes in those old mining towns along the Stanislaus, Feather and the American Rivers, you can see where they used hydraulic mining to blast away entire mountainsides. They made a real mess of that country before the farmers down in the Sacramento and San Joaquin valleys made a big fuss."

"Why?"

"Because hydraulic mining tore off the mountains and silted up all the western flowing rivers."

Peacock gazed out toward the distant mountains. "This looks like damned hard country to me. After taming Reno, I'd like to see California, especially San Diego, Sacramento and San Francisco."

"Well," Longarm said, "when you tire of Reno, you won't have that far to go to get to those places."

"Is there any gold or silver left on the Comstock Lode?"

"There was the last time I was up there, although I expect the big veins have about been worked out. Some of those shafts go down almost two thousand feet into Sun Mountain."

"Two thousand feet?" Peacock asked as if he couldn't believe his ears.

"That's right," Longarm told the man. "You see, in California, they mined the rivers and streams and that method of gold extraction was called 'placer mining.' But up on the Comstock Lode, there are no streams. In fact, they haul their water up to Virginia City and Gold Hill from Washoe Valley and up from the Walker River that runs through Carson City. On the Comstock Lode, the mining is done far underground. Oh, you'll see a lot of mine tailings from the little claims, but their production doesn't amount to much of anything compared to the really big mining companies that have the financial power to bore shafts and tunnels and holes deep into the mountain."

"How do the miners get down so deep?"

"They're lowered down on stout mine cables in cages."

Peacock shook his head. "Sounds dangerous."

"Everything about deep mining is dangerous," Longarm agreed. "There have been a lot of men that have died in those Comstock mines. Some take a misstep and plummet down the shafts, or the cables fray from overuse and break, sending a cage to the bottom. Or maybe there's some malfunction up above and the whole works collapses, sending miners to their deaths."

"What about cave-ins?"

"They happen all the time. Timber is so scarce up here that they have logged off much of the eastern slopes of the Sierras for a hundred miles north and south. One of the greatest dangers is for a miner to accidentally drive the head of his pick through a wall into a pocket of scalding water."

"Holy cow!" Peacock explained. "You mean they risk the chance of being boiled?"

"Yep." Longarm shifted in his seat. "But, if you go visit the main cemetery, you'll see that most of the men on the Comstock Lode die of pneumonia."

"It gets that cold up there?"

"It gets plenty cold in the winter. But mainly, when the shifts change and the miners are raised up from those hot depths, they are suddenly hit by icy winter winds. They catch pneumonia and die like flies."

"I'm glad I'm not a miner," Peacock said. "But I sure would like to go down in one of those mines at least once to see how it feels."

"You can arrange that," Longarm said. "For a price."

"Good." Peacock pointed up the line. "Say, that must be Elko."

"It is," Longarm told the man. "It's a rough and tumble ranching and rail town. There are lots of cowboys out in this country and some big cattle outfits. In this dry country, it takes a lot of range to feed a cow. There are also quite a few mustangs running wild out here. You might see a pen of them in the railroad stockyards."

"Will we hold over here?"

Longarm nodded. "Our train will take on wood and water. We'll have about an hour to take in the sights, but there really isn't much to see. Just cowboys, cows, horses and dogs."

"No women?" Peacock asked, not even trying to hide his disappointment. "I haven't had a woman since we left Denver."

"You'll live. But there is a red light district on the north side of the railroad tracks. It's rough."

Peacock looked more than a little interested. "And I suppose the women who work there are equally rough."

"That's right, but I have seen some lookers. The youngest and the prettiest, of course, command the highest prices. But then, you being a rich man, that shouldn't make any difference."

"It doesn't," Peacock said. "In fact, just as a gesture of goodwill, I'll be willing to treat you to one of them."

"No, thanks."

Peacock's face registered surprise. "Why not?"

"I've never had to pay for it and I never will. Just goes against my values, I guess."

"Those women have to make a living just like the rest of us," Peacock argued. "You can't hold that against them."

"I don't."

"Well, then?"

"Look," Longarm said. "I'll point you in the right direction. You won't have much time to dip your worm, but you won't be the only man on this train that will visit the painted ladies."

"I don't care if I'm the only one or not," Peacock said. "You think any of them are clean?"

"I have no idea. A man bent on paying for that kind of pleasure is always taking a chance."

"Sure he is," Peacock agreed, looking a bit put out. "But you can meet those kinds of women on any level of society. I could tell you stories about some of the wives of our United States congressmen that would curl your toes."

"I'll bet you could," Longarm said. "And I'll wager you sampled more than a few."

"Actually, I did. It always gave me an extra boot to take some rich old senator or congressman's wife or spoiled daughter to bed . . . often *his* bed. You may not believe this, but there's some fine looking women to be had in our capital."

"Is that what happened?"

He blinked. "What do you mean?"

"I mean," Longarm said, "is that why you were forced to leave Washington, D.C.?"

"Hell, no!" Peacock was annoyed. "Custis, I told you about Buffalo Bill and his Wild West Show."

"I remember. But I expect a lot of rich young men back East have seen that show and probably even read the dime novels thinking that they'd also like to go West and have great adventures. But they don't, because life back there is too easy. Now, in your case, I'm just wondering if you didn't get into a little trouble with a powerful man's wife or daughter that gave you the need to actually try your Western adventure."

"You are a very suspicious man. You're always looking for the dark secrets of others and have damn little faith in human nature."

"Not true," Longarm replied, halfway enjoying the way he'd put Peacock on the defensive. "I just know the values of most men and so very little surprises me. And that's why I'm quite sure that your decision to come West wasn't entirely voluntary."

Peacock had taken enough of Longarm's judgments. "I think I'll go back to my compartment and get ready for Elko."

"Rutherford, that's a good idea."

"But I'll be back when the train stops and take you up on your offer to show me around."

"That's fine. My offer stands."

The Easterner got up and hurried off, leaving Longarm to wonder exactly what the handsome young lawman had in mind.

• • •

"There sure isn't much here other than a few saloons and a whole lot of horses, cowboys and cattle," Peacock said after they'd walked down the main street, stopped and then turned back toward the tracks. "I wouldn't guess that more than five hundred people live here."

"That would be about right," Longarm told him. "Want a beer?"

"I have in mind something livelier. Point me to the best brothel in town."

"I don't know which that would be since I've never been in any of them," Longarm said. "But the Calico Cat seems to be the most popular, and I think it's that reddish orange house down this street."

"Sure you won't change your mind?"

Longarm shook his head. "Just be careful. Oh, and it would be best if you don't mention that you're a United States marshal."

"Why not? Are we supposed to be monks or something?"

"Nope. But we *are* supposed to be setting a high moral example. Just do as I say and keep your badge hidden and stay out of trouble. No fights and no shootings."

"Not unless I have to defend myself." Peacock almost smiled. "You wouldn't expect me to allow myself to be killed, would you?"

"I'm not worried about that possibility," Longarm told him. "And, if for some reason you need help, I'll be in the Red Dog Saloon over there nursing a beer."

"Okay."

Longarm turned and sauntered across the busy street. There were horses tied at the hitch rails and a lot of cowboys in the saloons or out on the boardwalk. Since Longarm was new and obviously no cowboy, he got plenty of notice.

The Red Dog Saloon had been around since the railroad had come through Elko in 1869, and it boasted that it had the coldest beer in Nevada as well as the best chili. Longarm had found both claims to be true. A man could have a couple of good beers and a huge bowl of excellent chili for less than a dollar and that was going to be a nice change from the bland railroad car food he'd been eating for days. Besides that, he'd become friends with the owner and bartender. Ike Foster was a short but powerful man who had been a buffalo hunter and then a bone picker on the plains of West Texas. He'd known Buffalo Bill Cody and worked with him for a few months and had also been in several skirmishes with the Comanche. He was known as a tough man and one not to be crossed under any circumstances.

"Marshal Long!" the man exclaimed, his grin without front teeth. "It's good to see you again."

"Same here, Ike."

"Cold beer?"

"Yep. And a bowl of chili with crackers."

"Comin' right up!"

Longarm took a chair over by the window and relaxed knowing that the cowboys who came into the Red Dog weren't going to be causing him or anyone else any trouble. Ike didn't stand for any troublemakers. If a cowboy got too rowdy, he was pitched out the door, often unconscious.

"So where are you heading this time?" Ike said, bringing over the beer and the chili and taking a seat at Longarm's table.

"Reno."

Longarm took a long swallow of the beer and smacked his lips with pleasure.

"Cold enough?" Ike asked.

"Sure is."

"Try the chili. I added some new spices and think it's better than ever. The boys say it's really got teeth."

Longarm lifted a spoonful to his mouth. Tears welled up in his eyes as he chewed, then swallowed.

"Too hot?"

"Nope. It's fine. I think it's an improvement," Longarm said, not wanting to hurt the man's feelings.

"Why are you going to Reno?"

"There's been some trouble there."

"Yeah. I heard about Marshal Deke Walker being ambushed," Ike said, shaking his head. "I knew Deke. He was a good man. Tough, but fair and honest."

"Yeah," Longarm said. "He was one of our best, and I considered him to be a personal friend."

"So is that why you're going there? To find out who shot him in the back?"

"That's a big part of it," Longarm admitted. "That, and introducing the town to its new marshal."

"Where is he?" Ike asked, looking around.

"He'll be along."

"If he's half the man that Deke was, then Reno will be lucky. Did you know that our town marshal quit just last week?"

"Is that right?"

"Yep. He make the mistake of putting some cowboys in jail and then going home to sleep while they tore it apart and escaped."

"Why didn't he go and arrest them again?"

"I think the man was ready to quit anyway and having his jail busted up was the last straw. He wasn't that good.

We've never had much luck finding lawmen. The truth is that Elko won't pay enough to attract a man with grit and good qualifications."

"I've heard that story all over the West," Longarm said. "Towns won't pay, and then they complain because they can't get a lawman who is experienced and honest."

"This one was experienced," Ike said, "but he sure wasn't honest. I think he was ready to go when he got into that trouble with those cowboys. One of them was the son of a very important rancher in these parts, and he'd have got the man fired if he hadn't resigned."

"It happens," Longarm said. "Any big news around here?"

"There was a pathetic attempt to hold up your west-bound train last week."

"Oh?"

"Yep," Ike said, "It happened about twenty miles west of Elko. Three men galloped up to the locomotive and pulled their guns and started yelling for the engineer to stop the train."

"Did he?"

"Nope. He had a gun of his own and a lot steadier platform to shoot off. Said he wounded one of them, and they quit and rode off to the north. I expect they learned their lessons the hard way. I hope the one that was shot died of lead poisoning out there in the sage someplace."

Ike had new customers so he left to work his bar. Longarm went back twice for refills of both chili and beer. After about thirty-five minutes, he was ready to get up and mosey on back to the train when up the street came Rutherford Peacock with a floozy on either arm.

"Oh, damn!" Longarm muttered, going out to meet Marshal Peacock.

"Hey, Custis! Look what I got for us to play with the rest of the way to Reno!"

Longarm wanted to duck between the buildings and hide, but Rutherford wasn't going to be ignored.

"We can have ourselves a good time. How far is it to Reno?"

"Too far," Longarm said as the man and his two women lurched up to stand before him with stupid grins on their faces.

"Custis, this is Rosie and Lizzie."

Longarm was surprised that they were better looking than the run-of-the-mill prostitutes you'd expect to find in a town this size. Both of them were short, probably only a little over five feet tall, blond and buxom. They also bore a strong resemblance to each other.

"We're sisters," Rosie said, hugging her sister. "I'm the youngest."

"You ain't either!" Lizzie argued. "Ma told us a thousand times if she told us once that you were born five minutes before me."

"Wasn't either."

"Was too!"

"Ladies," Rutherford said, pulling Lizzie away from her sister. "Our train is leaving, and we've got no time for arguments. Are you ready to come to Reno . . . or not?"

"But you didn't even give us time to pack a change of clothes!" Lizzie exclaimed.

"Yeah, but you did have time to get your money. Hell," Peacock said, "you can buy new outfits in Reno. I'll even buy them for you."

"You will?"

"Sure! So stop bellyaching and let's board the train. I can tell by the look on Custis's face he's getting worried about missing it."

"All right," Rosie said, slipping her arm around Longarm's waist and shoving him toward the station. "And anyway, it ain't like we got any good furniture or jewelry back at the Calico Cat. All we owned was some cheap trinkets and beauty aids that ain't worth worrying about 'cause these two handsome marshals are gonna take good care of us. Ain't that right?"

"We sure are," Peacock agreed, winking at Longarm. "We're going to take care of them just as soon as we can."

Lizzie giggled. "You bad, bad boys!"

"I'm not taking care of them," Longarm said, removing Rosie's arm. "I'll have my hands full as it is when we get to Reno. For that matter, Marshal Peacock, so will you."

He scoffed. "Don't be a spoilsport, Custis. After all, we're not *marrying* these lovely sisters. We're just riding them to Reno."

The girls had high-pitched and irritating laughs, but when Rosie put her arms back around Longarm and gave him a big smack on the lips and a tweak on his privates ... Well, Custis decided that no one was perfect and that he might as well enjoy the feminine company during the last leg of their railroad trip.

"The train is about to pull out," Longarm said. "Let's go if we're going to, but just remember that I can't afford to treat these girls to much of anything."

"Don't worry," Peacock assured him. "I'll take care of it."

"I'll bet you will," Longarm said, turning and starting for the train.

Rosie hauled herself up close. "Don't you know how to treat a pretty woman?"

"Sometimes I do." He was miffed at Rutherford Peacock and it must have shown.

"I could be mistaken, but I don't think you even like Marshal Peacock."

"Whatever gave you that idea?"

"He said that you might not take up with me or my sister. Said you'd never paid for a woman. So he decided that he'd pay for you both. I don't understand why you're acting so huffy."

"I'm not being huffy," Longarm argued. "I just like to make my own decisions about who I meet and what I do. That's all."

"Well," Rosie said. "If you don't want to be around me, just say so, and I'll leave you alone. Our mother lives in Reno, and we're going back home to take care of her before she dies. I don't think she's got long to live, but she might hang on a few more years. She's a tough, old bird . . . crabby as a teased snake, but she has a nice, big house. A Victorian in the best part of town. Me and Lizzie are going to inherit it, so we'll have a place all our own."

"Glad to hear that."

"We might make some money in that house," Rosie said. "It's a nice neighborhood and there are some successful men around there that look like they could use more fun in their lives."

"Are you saying you're going to use the house to entertain customers?"

"Why not? A couple of girls like us have to make their livings somehow, don't we?"

"I expect there are lots of ways to do that other than spreading your legs. You ever think about marriage and family?"

Rosie looked shocked. "You mean like becoming respectable housewives and mothers?"

"Yeah, something like that."

"Forget it," Rosie told him. "I've saw what happened

to all the girls we grew up with that got married. They're already fat and miserable. They all have husbands who cheat on them and kids that drive 'em half crazy. That's definitely not what Lizzie and I want out of life."

"What do you want?"

Rosie gave his question a moment of thought, and then said with a laugh in her voice, "We want a pair of big, handsome fellers like you and Rutherford!" She leaned over and pinched him between the legs again and laughed uproariously.

Despite himself, Longarm couldn't help but like the brazen little woman. Rosie was without pretext and she made no excuses or apologies for who she was and what she wanted to become.

"You're not married, are you?"

"No."

"I can't imagine why not," she said as they reached the train just as it was starting to roll.

All four of them jumped on board and Peacock said, "Give us an hour and then we'll trade coaches. You're going to need my compartment."

"Why don't you ask the conductor to give me one of my own in first class?" Longarm asked. "It shouldn't cost much."

"Good idea," he said. "Better yet, you do it."

Peacock shoved money into Longarm's pocket and headed up the aisle with Lizzie.

"How much did he give us?" Rosie asked.

Longarm extracted the money and counted it. "Fifty dollars."

"That should do it," she said.

"I guess it should at that," Longarm told her, deciding to swallow his pride and take Rosie into first class.

A private compartment cost him only thirty dollars, because it wasn't all that far to Reno, maybe a little over three hundred miles.

"This is real nice," Rosie said when they settled in and began to undress. "You gonna let me see any of the country between here and Reno?"

"There's not much to see," Longarm told her. "Just sage and those barren hills and a few peaks."

Rosie gazed out the window for a moment and then she closed her hand on Longarm's manhood. "Yeah, you're right. *Your* peak is far more interesting."

"Glad you think so," he said, lifting her hips and then impaling her on his rod.

"Oh, yes," she cooed as she started to move up and down.

"Just lay still and let the motion of the train do our work," he told her. "It's slow but it'll drive you wild."

"Is that right? You mean we just relax?"

"That's right."

So Rosie lay on him and closed her eyes. After a few miles, she was beginning to understand what he meant.

"Oh, my! This *is* nice!"

"I told you so," Longarm answered. "I'll give us another twenty miles."

"You talk like you've done this before on a train."

"As often as I can," he said with a grin.

Rosie squeezed her eyes shut, but Longarm could feel her heart pounding faster than the wheels on the track. "I got a feeling that you're not going to be able to do this even another five miles," he said.

Her fingernails dug into his hard buttocks and she giggled, "Marshal, you sure got that right!"

Two miles later, Rosie was screaming and humping like a crazy woman, and Longarm was grinning from ear to ear.

Chapter 7

About twenty-five miles west of Elko and five miles after Longarm and Rosie had reached their shuddering bliss in the little first-class compartment, three horsemen appeared out of nowhere. One of them wore a sling on his left arm and was firing his gun with his right hand while holding his reins in his teeth. This time, before opening fire at the locomotive engineer, the train robbers had picked a section of the track that rose steeply up a long grade.

Longarm threw Rosie aside, then grabbed his pants. Because of the lack of space and the train now rounding a bend, he had trouble getting dressed and buckling on his gunbelt. Rosie got wedged in between the sleeper and the wall and couldn't get unstuck.

"Help!" Rosie cried, appendages waving like a turtle turned on its back. "You almost stepped on me and I can't . . . get . . . up!"

"Sorry," he apologized, grabbing her outstretched arms and hauling her to her feet. "Sounds like the train is being attacked."

"Don't get shot!" she yelled as Longarm burst out of the private compartment barefooted. The train was already in chaos with passengers shouting and yelling as if they were being slaughtered. Longarm bulled his way up the aisle. He heard gunfire that seemed to be originating from up near the locomotive and hoped he wasn't too late to help the engineer.

In the front coach, his progress was stopped when he came upon a very large man who was pale, shaky and having difficulty getting his breath. The huge man was in great distress and blocking the entire aisle. Longarm thought maybe he was having heart trouble so he took a few more precious seconds to try and calm him down and get him back into his sleeping compartment. It was like trying to push a horse into an outhouse.

"Someone help this man!" Longarm shouted. "Is there a doctor on this train?"

The conductor appeared, face ashen and blood seeping through his coat. "There's no doctor on board that I know of," he gasped, looking as if his own heart might quit.

Longarm could still hear shots over the pounding of the tracks. "What's going on?"

"Your friend managed to reach the locomotive, and it's a good thing, because our engineer is dead and so is our fireman. There's a lot of lead flying, and I tried to help the marshal but took a bullet."

Just then, the fat man grabbed his chest and his heels began to drum on the hard aisle. Suddenly, he stiffened and then went limp.

"He's dead," Longarm said, quickly checking the man's pulse and looking up at the wounded conductor. "How bad are you hit?"

"I don't know."

The man sagged into a chair and a woman two seats back began to scream as if her throat were being cut. As bad as Longarm wanted to get up to the locomotive and help Peacock, he couldn't leave the conductor to bleed to death. Not if the man still had a chance of being saved.

"Just take it easy," Longarm told the man as he opened his coat and studied the terrible bullet wound.

"Marshal Long, tell me the truth, am I going to die?"

"Not if I can get this bleeding stopped."

"I *can't* die," the conductor whispered. "I'm only forty-six and I've still got kids to raise. Three of them! Don't let me bleed to death, Marshal! Don't leave me."

"I'm not going anywhere until we get the bleeding stopped. Just hold on and don't give up on us!"

Rosie and Lizzie suddenly appeared and both were only partially dressed. "What can we do to help?"

"Get some bandages!" Longarm shouted. "Anything to stop the bleeding."

The sisters weren't the kind to panic at the sight of blood like most of the other passengers. Without hesitation, they removed the last of their underclothing and handed it over to Longarm. The woman who had been screaming fainted at the sight of their naked bodies. Young men and old men gaped and children's eyes grew round with wonder, but Longarm didn't care and neither did Lizzie or Rosie.

"It looks like the bullet missed his lungs," Longarm said as he unbuttoned the conductor's blood-soaked shirt and pressed a pair of pink panties hard against the bullet hole.

"I'm dying!" the conductor sobbed, grabbing Lizzie's bare leg. "Oh, I feel as if I'm leaving this world!"

"Hang on!" Longarm shouted into the man's pale and contorted face. "I'm going to stop the bleeding, and you still have a chance."

"Please don't give up on us," Rosie begged. "You got to fight hard or you'll die."

The conductor's eyes had been shut, but now they popped open and he stared at Rosie. "Are you . . . an angel?" he rasped.

"No, honey. I'm just a whore, but I still want you to live."

The conductor seemed confused and then his eyes swung over to Lizzie and he said, "I'm seeing double. Four big tits, the faces of two angels. Pastor Wilson never said it would be like this! What . . ."

"He's delirious," Lizzie said to her sister. "I don't think he's going to make it."

Rosie sniffled and placed the conductor's hand on her bare breast. "Poor, poor little man."

Longarm grunted. "I think we're getting the bleeding stopped. If he's not bleeding too bad inside, he could still make it. I just wish we had a doctor on board."

A new volley of gunfire caught everyone's attention. Longarm rose to his feet and reached for his six-gun. "I can't do anything more for the conductor. Not right now, at least."

"We'll hold the bandage tight," Lizzie said. "Go help Rutherford before they kill him."

"All right," Longarm said. "Keep the bandage pressed tight and keep him quiet. There's a good doctor in Elko, and we can back the train up and see if we can still save the man's life."

"But he's turning gray!" Rosie cried.

Longarm had seen this happen before and it wasn't a good sign. Not good at all. "The man is going into shock. That may be the death of him, but I can't say for sure. I've got to go help Peacock. I'll be back just as soon as I can, and don't anybody leave this car until I do. We're going to be all right!"

Longarm threw himself up the aisle and when he

reached the end of the coach, he tore open the door and found himself facing the coal tender car. He climbed its ladder and when he reached the top, threw himself into the pile of coal that was being used to fuel the locomotive's boiler. Choking and hacking coal dust, he half crawled, half tumbled down the pile and landed in the locomotive as black as a tar baby but still holding his gun.

Peacock was crouched behind a metal plate, and he was nearly as black as Longarm. "What took you so long? I'm out of ammunition."

"Never mind," Longarm said, wiping the dust from his eyes. "How many?"

"I shot one off his horse. There are just two left, but they must have extra weapons."

Longarm wiped his dust-covered gun on his dust-covered pants. He grabbed a piece of steel and raised to a crouch knowing that he had five bullets to kill two men. Trouble was, Longarm was being tossed about like dice in a cup, so that it was going to be almost impossible to shoot accurately.

When Longarm's head lifted above the cover of the locomotive's cab, the horsemen opened up and one of their errant bullets ricocheted wildly off a piece of metal and sent him sprawling. He slammed into the boiler and his gun was knocked from his hand. The Colt revolver spun across the floor and would have been lost except that Peacock scooped it up and returned fire.

"Got 'em."

Longarm struggled to his feet, vision still blurred by the coat of gritty dust in his eyes. "You got them both?"

"That's right! Look!"

Through stinging tears, Longarm squinted and saw two riderless horses running hard beside the train. He leaned out of the cab and gazed back down the tracks to see two still bodies sprawled on the ground. He also noticed that their train had topped a ridge and that the grade was now slanting steeply downward and they were quickly gathering speed.

Far too much speed.

"There's a curve at the bottom of this grade!" Longarm shouted. With growing desperation, he turned his eyes to the steam locomotive's gauges, valves, wheels and handles. His eyes came to rest on the throttle, which he figured was all the way open. Longarm made the adjustment and he felt the train slow but they were still going far too fast down the track.

"Peacock, do you know anything about running a locomotive?"

"Not yet!"

Peacock handed Longarm back his gun and grabbed what he hoped was a brake. "Hang on!" he yelled pulling hard but not feeling any results.

Longarm grabbed the brake and helped as he shouted, "We can't slow this thing down enough to keep it on the track when we hit that turn down at the bottom!"

"Do tell!" Peacock yelled, his smile wolfish. "Then I guess we better figure out what to do pretty damn quick!"

"We need to let off steam . . . quick!"

Together, they started turning and adjusting valves and anything else that looked like it might slow their breakneck momentum.

"Got it!" Peacock shouted over the roar and pounding of steel tracks against wheels. "Feel us slowing?"

Longarm nodded, eyes glued on the turn at the bottom of the long grade. He didn't know much about trains or tracks, but he sure hoped that they didn't derail. If that happened, a lot of people were going to die.

"Hang on!" Longarm shouted as the locomotive swept

into the curve. He could feel it lean and then . . . it seemed to hang suspended for an instant before Longarm heard a tremendous *bang!* The locomotive, steam spewing from what must have been some emergency valves, shuddered, righted itself and charged on through the bend, iron wheels shrieking in protest.

Longarm couldn't see because of all the steam, smoke and the coal tender being between himself and the first passenger coach. But he could feel the entire train being wrenched through the curve and, after what seemed an eternity, they hit a straightaway on flat ground.

"Let's see if we can get it stopped!" Peacock shouted.

"All right!"

They leaned against the brake, muscles straining, and then they released the steam valve and a huge cloud exploded out of the boiler as the locomotive slowly came to a shuddering halt.

"I thought we were goners for certain," Longarm said, almost limp from exhaustion.

"Me, too," Peacock told him, face blackened and streaming with sweat. "Do I look as bad as you do?"

"Probably worse."

"Impossible."

Longarm wanted nothing more than to stand on solid earth. He climbed down and, on wobbly knees, began to march back down the line of cars.

"Custis!" Rosie cried, flying off the train and running down the tracks, still naked, to throw herself into his arms. "You saved us!"

Longarm hugged her tight and then he pushed her back and removed his dirty coat. "Better put this on."

For the first time, the woman seemed to realize that she was indecent. "Oh my gosh! Is . . . is Lizzie like this?"

"Last time I saw her she was."

"Oh my *gosh*!" She screeched as Lizzie came running toward them.

Longarm tore off his shirt, which was ruined by sweat and the coal dust, and handed it to Lizzie.

"Is Rutherford still alive?" she asked.

"He sure is. You'll find him up in the locomotive."

Lizzie took off running.

"You're both heroes," Rosie said. "We saw those train robbers fall from their horses. You killed them all."

"Actually," Longarm confessed. "It was Rutherford that shot them with my gun."

"Oh."

Longarm gazed back down the tracks. "What about the conductor? If he's still alive, we probably ought to try and back this thing all the way to Elko but . . ."

"He's dead," Rosie told him as tears welled up in her eyes. "He died in my arms, and there wasn't a thing I could do to help. I feel so bad for him and his family."

"Me, too," Longarm said. "But it could have been a whole lot worse if the train had overturned at high speed trying to make that bend at the bottom of the tracks. We nearly went over."

"We could feel the train lift on the high side, and I thought we were finished," Rosie told him. "The wheels were screeching so loud that I thought I'd lose my mind. What are we going to do now?"

Longarm reached into the coat that Rosie was wearing and found a handkerchief. He slowly wiped the grit and dust from around his eyes and his mouth. "I sure could use a drink," he said. "That was a close shave for everyone."

"Let's go back to the car and find you something," Rosie said.

But Longarm shook his head. "I'd better go back up to

the locomotive and see if we can get it moving again. Anyone else hurt in the cars?"

"I don't know. Some of the women and children were screaming and nearly hysterical. I saw passengers being thrown around like rag dolls, and I'm sure that several were injured . . . but probably not seriously."

"We'll push on," Longarm told her as he studied the precipitous grade they'd just descended. "I sure don't want to back this whole train up that grade."

"Where is the next big town?"

"It's Reno," he said. "We got maybe three hundred miles to go, so we ought to be there in six or seven hours . . . provided we can get the steam back up and keep it rolling."

"Maybe there's someone back in the coaches that knows how to operate a locomotive."

"Maybe," Longarm said. "Let's go have a drink, get you dressed and find out."

Forty-five minutes later Rosie, Longarm and a grizzled old railroad engineer who had been on his way to Sacramento marched up the tracks to find Lizzie and Peacock sitting beside the locomotive. Like Longarm, Peacock had removed his coat and given it to the naked woman and his arm was draped across her shoulders.

"We made it," Peacock said, coming to his feet. "We pulled it off pretty fine."

Longarm nodded. "We made a good team," he admitted.

"And we'll make an even better one in Reno."

"Maybe so." Longarm turned to see the old railroad man staring longingly at Lizzie's still exposed breasts. "You think you can do it?"

"Could I ever," he breathed, licking his lips.

"Not her, the locomotive!" Longarm snapped. "Can you get us to Reno?"

"Not a problem," the man said, tearing his eyes away from Lizzie. "It ain't been that many years since I ran one of these things. We used wood, but that don't matter. I'm going to need to take on water a time or two up ahead, and I'll need someone to shovel coal."

"I'll do it," Longarm offered.

"And I'll help you," Peacock said. "One thing for sure, we can't get any dirtier than we already are."

Longarm grinned because that was sure the truth.

Chapter 8

Reno, Nevada, had once been called Lake's Crossing. During the time of the California Gold Rush and for several years afterward, it had been the place where overland pioneers had stopped to rest and fatten up their weary livestock before tackling the difficult Sierra Nevadas at Donner Pass. Some California-bound wagon trains, like the Donner Party, had died because they'd waited too long before making the climb and been caught in the deep snows and ferocious blizzards that swept across the Sierras, sometimes as early as October.

With the discovery of gold and silver on the Comstock Lode in 1858, thousands of miners had poured back over the Sierras from California, and they panned out streams and rivers. Others had come from distant places around the world, lured by the almost unheard of wages of three dollars a day being offered for skilled hard-rock miners. The best were from Wales, but they'd come from as far away as Australia to get rich.

Now, however, with the Comstock mines starting to yield less ore production each year, Reno was coming into its own as an important ranching, lumber and railroad town. It was true that the Comstock Lode had consumed much of the eastern slope forests and that the Truckee River was badly silted from dredging, but the people of Reno were more than confident that their city would prosper and endure, unlike so many other boom-and-bust mining towns that had come and gone along both sides of the mighty Sierras.

Rutherford Peacock was all eyes as he leaned out of the coach window and studied the upcoming town. He took in the grassy valley and saw the sparkle of the river gleaming like a ribbon of silver in the setting sun. His eyes lifted to the towering peaks, several of which were still mantled by snow.

"It's the handsomest town I've yet seen in Nevada," he declared loudly, but to no one in particular. "What's the population?"

"Two or three thousand," an officious man in his fifties answered. "But half of them are outlaws, drunks, whores or misfits."

Peacock retracted his head from the great outdoors and leaned back in his chair. "I don't believe that."

"Well, it's the truth. Reno is the Biblical Gomorrah, only it's in the West. Why, if there isn't at least one gunfight and killing a day, the populace starts to feeling they've been cheated."

Peacock glanced over at Longarm. "Is he telling the truth or exaggerating?"

"I think he's exaggerating . . . but maybe not by much," Longarm replied. "It's not hard to believe that, since Marshal Walker's murder, Reno is a wild and dangerous town."

The man nodded in agreement. "Deke Walker was the best, and while he was alive, this place was decent for women and children. But all that has changed for the worse."

"Then why are you coming back?" Peacock asked the well-dressed and opinionated man.

"Because I own a merchantile business. Take my advice young man, if you're going to try and take Marshal Walker's place, you'd better be prepared to walk tall and shoot straight. And you'd better have a set of eyes in the back of your head."

Peacock didn't look too worried. "I'll be fine. Marshal Long is going to watch my back for at least a few days before he visits the Comstock Lode. Isn't that right, Custis?"

"Yeah, I'll do that," Longarm promised. "I'll stick around until we see which way the wind is blowing and take care of anyone who might like to see you end up like my friend Deke."

The merchantile owner nodded sagely. "Maybe with the two of you walking a beat and cracking heads, you can get the job done. But I wouldn't bet on it. The day after Marshal Walker was ambushed, some of the saloon and brothel owners held a real celebration. Free drinks at the bar and all the pickles, pork feet and crackers you could eat."

Longarm couldn't help but bristle at this news. "Have you got a paper and pencil handy?"

"Of course."

"Write down the names of those businesses that celebrated Deke Walker's death."

"No, thanks," the merchant said, starting to put away his writing materials. "If word got out that I did that for the law, I could be their next target."

Longarm reached across the aisle and grabbed the merchant by the lapel. "Mister," he said, voice hard as nails, "if you don't do as I say, I swear that you're going to wish you had never laid eyes on me or Marshal Peacock."

"Are you threatening *me*?"

"I ain't paying you a compliment," Longarm growled, twisting the man's collar up tight around his neck so that his face started to turn crimson. "Now, do as I say and no one gets hurt."

The man nodded his double chins and bristled with righteous indignation. He retrieved his pad and pencil, and his hand was shaking badly as he began to compile a list.

Peacock raised his eyebrows in question, then said, "And *I'm* supposed to be the one with the temper?"

Longarm didn't dignify the question with a civil reply, but when their train rolled into Reno, he had his list and he knew most of the offending businesses. Some of them were a surprise, others he could have predicted would be jubilant that law and order had finally been routed so that lawlessness could prevail.

"Where are we staying?" Peacock asked with Lizzie hanging on his arm at the train depot.

"There are plenty of hotels in town," Longarm told the man. "I think we should room in different places."

Peacock looked surprised. "Why?"

"Two targets in the same place are a lot easier to hit than if they're separated. Besides that, I don't want to steal your thunder."

"My thunder?"

"It's your deal," Longarm told the Easterner. "You're the town's new federal marshal. The jail is about two blocks down Virginia Street past the Truckee River. I'll be seeing you tomorrow. In the meantime, be careful, and watch your back. Once the word gets out that you're Walker's replacement, the same people that killed him will want to kill you."

"You make it sound like there are a lot of them."

"There might be. We'll find out soon enough."

"Custis, honey!" Rosie cried. "Are you just up and leaving us?"

Longarm felt a pang of guilt, but he knew that he needed to sever the relationship if he were to be effective. He hoped that Peacock could see the wisdom of doing the same. It just wasn't right for the town's marshal to arrive with a woman of low virtue hanging all over him. Hypocritical or not, it set a bad example and first impressions were critical.

"Rosie," he said, "it's been nice. And I'm sure that we'll meet again before I leave town, but I've got to work alone. I've been here before, and I've made enemies as well as friends. Like the former marshal, I've been shot at from ambush but was lucky enough to survive. Being with me would be dangerous for you so . . . good-bye and good luck."

Rosie appeared crestfallen but she had too much pride to beg. "All right, Custis. Just take care of yourself and, if you get the need to . . . well, you know what we were like together on that train . . . you can have it from me anytime for free."

Longarm couldn't help but grin, and despite the fact that there were people about, he took the young woman in his arms and gave her a far from brotherly kiss before he grabbed his bags and headed up the street.

Reno hadn't changed much since his last visit. But then, he calculated, that had been only five months ago. It was a nice town, and as he strolled over the bridge on Virginia Street and gazed down at the swift-flowing Truckee River, he saw mallards quacking and begging passersby to throw food down to them. And a short way upriver, three teenage boys were swimming in a water hole and having a fine time splashing each other and skipping flat rocks across the roiling river's surface.

Yes sir, Longarm thought, *this is a fine little town, and I sure hope that we live long enough to clean it up and restore law and order.*

And as he passed over the bridge heading south toward a rooming house where he was treated as a special guest, Longarm couldn't help but remember a not-too-long-past spring day when he and the beautiful Miss Dolly Reardon had strolled along the riverfront feeding those very same ducks. He wondered if she had gotten married, and he hoped not, although he wasn't sure why. Dolly had been pretty special and, had it not been for her meddling, overbearing father, Longarm would have been tempted to try a new line of work here in Nevada.

Oh well, he thought, *I guess I did the right thing.*

Marshal Peacock was hurt that Longarm had temporarily deserted him and, as he watched the man walk away, he felt irritation and disappointment.

"Some friend," Lizzie said to him, her brow knitted with disapproval.

"Well," Peacock replied, "he's the kind of man that could either be your very good friend or your worst enemy. After what we went through with that runaway train, I thought we'd already become friends."

"Think again," Rosie told him. "Say, do you want to meet our mother? She's real old and not too good in the head, but there's plenty of empty rooms in the house. I'm sure that we could find you a bed."

"Thanks, but no thanks," Peacock replied, thinking that Longarm might have a point about being seen with a pair of good-hearted but obviously working prostitutes. "I'd better find my own living place."

"Well," Lizzie said, "can you at least come by to visit us?"

"Of course!" He smiled and kissed them both on their cheeks. "I'm going to be real busy for the next few days trying to get things sorted out. But I'll come by once I get things organized and under control."

"We live on Second Street in a big two-story Victorian with a balcony off the front and red rosebushes all over the porch."

"I'll remember that," he told them. "You girls run along now. I've got to go visit my new office and inspect the jail."

"Don't get killed before you come to visit," Lizzie told him.

"I wouldn't think of it," Peacock replied as he headed off in the same direction that Longarm had taken only a few moments ago.

When he found the office, he was surprised to see a teenager standing on a wooden box painting over the words U.S. MARSHAL'S OFFICE with dark brown paint.

"Hey!" Peacock called as he approached. "What in blazes are you doing?"

The paint-splattered kid was tall and gangly with ragged bib overalls and a pimpled face. His eyes were closely set together and he had bat ears. All in all, he was one of the homeliest kids Peacock had ever laid eyes upon.

"Why I'm painting over this here sign," he snapped back.

"I can see that. How come?"

"On account of we ain't got no sheriff nor U.S. marshal anymore and this here is about to become a law office."

"Is that right?"

"Yes, it is," the kid said, starting to dip his paintbrush in his can and go back to work. "Now, I got no more time to talk."

Peacock didn't like to be dismissed by anyone, especially an ugly kid with bad manners, so he kicked the box out from under his feet. The kid spilled over and his can of white paint upended on his chest and covered the lower half of his face.

"What . . . what'd you do that for?" the teenager cried, hurling the can aside and jumping to his feet with his fists wet with paint but clenched.

"I did it because you're lacking in manners, and because I've been sent here to take over as the town's federal marshal. And I expect you to get back up on that box and fix that sign with my name on it."

The teenager wiped paint from his mouth and chin with his forefinger, then slung it to the ground. "Dammit! You could have just told me so instead of kicking the box out like that. Look at the awful mess I made of myself and this here boardwalk!"

Peacock had no sympathy. "Go home, clean up and come back here to put my name on that sign."

The kid sniffled and wiped his wet hands on his dirty pants. "You ruined a good can of paint. Now I'm gonna have to buy more and money don't grow on trees in this town. I ain't got no money for more paint."

Peacock reached into pocket and tossed the kid a handful of change. "Who was the attorney?"

"You mean the one that was going to rent this office?"

"That's right."

"His name is Douglas Bunch." The teenager's eyes narrowed. "And I'll tell you this much, he's going to sue you for everything you got or ever will have when he hears about what you did to me."

"Is that right?"

"Yes, it is. And I'm going to go tell him right now!"

If not for a small crowd that had gathered to watch the interesting proceedings, Peacock would have booted the kid in the rear end and sent him sprawling once again. But since he was the new marshal, he restrained himself and managed to say, "Tell Douglas to come and see me right away. And, if you don't come back and fix that sign, I'll hunt you down and throw you in jail."

"For doin' what I was paid to do? Ha! You sure ain't gonna last long in this town, Marshal. You sure as hell ain't, and I hope you get the same lead poisoning that Deke Walker got. Yes, sir, I sure . . ."

Peacock drew his pistol and pointed it at the teenager's crotch. "You're so ugly you probably never had a chance to use what hangs between your legs. But if you don't shut up and do as I've told you, you'll *never* get a chance to know a woman."

And just to emphasize his point, Peacock sent a round between the kid's skinny legs and watched him jump a good three feet straight up into the air. When the kid landed, he whirled and took off running like a scared jackrabbit.

"Damn but I can't tolerate a mouthy, ugly boy like that," he muttered as he carefully skirted the spilled paint and went around to the office door. It was unlocked and Peacock went inside, then closed the door and had a good look around.

He'd read enough dime novels to have formed an idea of what a real frontier marshal or sheriff's office would look like, and this one entirely filled the bill. It wasn't neat and it wasn't clean but there were WANTED posters tacked to the walls and two scarred desks and chairs. He looked with approval upon the small, but no doubt important, potbellied stove with its bent and blackened chimney pipe. Beyond that, at the rear of the building, was a jail cell.

"It'll do," Peacock said, moving slowly across the small office and hearing his boot heels thump on the rough plank floor. When he reached the jail cell, he gripped the bars and gave them a powerful yank. They felt solid, and the little wooden prisoner's bunk, with its pitiful straw mattress, was exactly like the one he'd read about in his favorite dime novel, *Shootin' Six-gun Sheriff*.

Yes sir, Marshal Rutherford Peacock thought with satisfaction as he took a seat and threw his boots up on what had been Deke Walker's desk, *this will do just fine for now*.

Chapter 9

"So what the hell is the meaning of this outrage?" the dumpy lawyer with a cheap cigar stuffed into his mouth cried as he burst into the office. "Just who do you think you are, attacking Thad Wilson and causing him grievous insult, not to mention an injury."

Peacock barely raised his glance from the stack of WANTED posters he'd been enjoying, but when he spoke, his voice was hard. "That kid is insulting, and the only injury he suffered was to his pride."

"Marshal . . . if you really are a United States marshal . . . I might have to take you before Judge Evans and show you that we do not tolerate abusive behavior toward women, children, dogs or animals of any kind."

Peacock came to his feet, and then he walked over to the irate lawyer and jerked the smelly cigar out of his mouth. He opened the door and pitched the stinking stogie, then the lawyer into the street. "Next time you come through that door, you'd better remember your manners and show the law here in Reno some *respect*."

The lawyer climbed unsteadily to his feet, jaw hanging down in astonishment. He spat shreds of tobacco and wagged his forefinger at Peacock. "I am going to sue you for . . . for defamation of character and aggravated assault!"

"You can sue me for whatever you want you country clod, but I'll countersue you for threatening a federal officer and trespassing."

"Trespassing?"

"That's right."

"That's *my* office you're standing in! I paid the city clerk twenty dollars for the first month's rent."

"Then I suggest you ask for a refund," Rutherford said. "This is the marshal's office and a jail. Furthermore, I'm not only the new federal marshal, but I also happen to be a university-trained attorney at law who passed the New York bar with honors, while I'd be willing to bet that the only bar *you* ever passed was sitting in a low-class saloon."

The attorney was still sputtering his ridiculous threats when Peacock slammed the door and went back to his reading.

Thirty minutes later, there was a firm knock on his door. Peacock hollered, "If you've come back to apologize, then you may open the door. If not, then go away."

"It's Judge Evans, and I apologize to no one!"

Peacock's feet had been up on the desk, but now he suddenly dropped them and hurried over to open the door. The judge was a tall, but somewhat infirm, gentleman in his late sixties with a silver mane, a thick mustache and matching goatee. He looked very distinguished.

"Come in, Judge." Peacock stuck out his hand and introduced himself.

The judge ignored the proffered hand and closed the door behind him. Without any word of welcome, he said, "Let me see your badge and papers of authority."

"Of course. You'll see that the papers are in order and signed by the federal commissioners both in Washington, D.C., as well as in Denver."

The judge took his time reading the documents and when he was finished, his stern expression softened and handed them back saying, "I was in Washington, D.C., once . . . but that was long before you were even born. I used to like to love the color and the perfume of the apple blossoms. How's the old town looking these days?"

"Splendid. I was there last year and they were enlarging the halls of Congress."

"Hmmm," the judge mused, "I think that I'd like to return once more. I remember the theaters, the music halls, gardens and high fashion of the ladies and the gentlemen. My late wife, Beatrice, bless her soul, was from Washington, D.C. She always blamed me for taking her out West. Never did like it and, if I hadn't been such a selfish, self-centered bastard, I'd have taken her back to the East twenty years ago. She was quite a beauty in her day, you know."

"I'm sure she was. Just as I'm sure you also cut quite a handsome figure."

The judge smiled and was obviously susceptible to flattery. "I was as handsome as you are, Marshal. How tall are you?"

"A shade over six foot four."

"So was I. But, as you can see, age and the responsibility of judging men guilty of crimes that demand they forfeit their lives has taken its physical toll. And what about you?"

"Sir?"

"Responsibility. Are you man enough to handle the responsibility of being a frontier marshal? *Our* new federal marshal?"

The question, and the grave way it was posed, momentarily caught Peacock off guard, but he quickly recovered. "Judge, with all my heart, I believe I am."

"Well, we shall see. Marshal . . . Peacock?"

"Yes. Rutherford Peacock, at your service."

"Unusual name, but perhaps fitting. Anyway, Marshal Peacock, I'm sure that I don't have to tell you that your predecessor, Marshal Walker, was an outstanding lawman."

"Yes, sir. I've already heard that many times."

Evans shook his head sadly. "And that he was assassinated by some cowardly ambusher?"

"Yes, I heard that as well."

"Then you must know that your own life is in some degree of mortal danger. Poor Marshal Walker might have been gunned down by someone with a more . . . shall we say . . . sinister and complicated motive than mere revenge."

"I understand. Judge, won't you have a seat? I'm going to replace the furniture, but for now, this will have to do."

"Why would you replace this furniture?"

"It sets a bad tone," Peacock replied. "If someone comes in here and sees that this place is disorderly and everything looks as if it has been cast off, then it sets a bad tone, and I get little respect."

Peacock winked as if confiding in an old and trusted friend. "A man's surroundings do reflect his character, don't you think?"

The judge nodded thoughtfully. "Yes, you make a very good point. Unfortunately, I doubt that there are sufficient public funds for replacing much of anything in this office."

"No matter," Peacock said offhandedly, "I'll replace the desks and filing cabins, the chairs and other furniture with my own funds."

His gray eyebrows lifted with surprise. "Hmmm, has the

federal government increased their wages all of a sudden?"

"No, I have my own money."

"Which is to say that you are a well-heeled lawman?"

"I have been blessed financially."

"Well," the judge said with a broad smile, "that is excellent news. Then I won't have to worry about you robbing the cowboys and workingmen of Reno when they've had too much to drink and go to sleep in the alley."

"No," Peacock replied. "You certainly won't."

"Good." The judge hobbled stiffly over to a chair and took a seat. "Tell me about yourself. Douglas Bunch, the man you tossed out of this office and who filed a complaint with me, said you claimed to be a university-educated attorney of law."

"I am. University of New York. Third in my class, and I passed the bar exam in the upper two percent."

"Impressive. And, if it isn't too personal, how did you come by your money?"

Peacock told him about his inheritance and then said, "Now, tell *me* something, Judge Evans. Other than some vengeance-minded individual, who would want to kill Marshal Walker?"

"Plenty of people. But we can discuss that over dinner tonight for which I thank you in advance."

"My pleasure," Peacock replied, knowing who was going to be paying for the best and most expensive dinner in Reno.

The judge stood up and looked around. "Yes," he said, "this office is a disgrace, and I just happen to have a very nice rolltop desk, chair and filing cabinet that would really spruce things up nicely. Marshal, I can let you have all three of those quality pieces for . . . hmmm . . . let's say a hundred dollars."

"That would be a great favor to me."

"You can come by and inspect them first."

"Not necessary," Peacock told the old schemer, knowing he'd just bought something much more valuable than office furniture.

"Excellent! I'll be going now. We can meet at the Berkley House at seven. They have a fine selection of wines. Since you're buying, I'll let you choose, but I do prefer the French cabernet."

"That's my favorite as well."

The judge got up and spied a cigar that Rutherford had laid on the desk. "Why, I declare. That looks like it might be a very good cigar."

"It is."

"Cuban?"

"Havana's best. Would you like one?"

"I believe I would."

Peacock handed him the cigar, and when it was ready to be smoked, he even lit it for the judge, who inhaled deeply, then sighed with contentment. "I haven't had one this good since I left the East coast. How much did it cost?"

"A dollar."

"Worth every penny. They're especially wonderful with an after dinner brandy, you know."

"Yes, they are. I'll be sure to bring a couple that we can enjoy over our brandy."

"Tell me, was your father a wealthy man?"

"Not at all. He was a New York City policeman. He never had much money, but he was highly respected. He was my model and, for a time, I followed in his footsteps."

"As a big city policeman?"

"That's right."

"How interesting. So why didn't you practice law or stay on the New York City police force?"

Peacock shrugged his broad shoulders. "I guess I just

got restless and had to come out and experience the American West. I thought it to be the place of greatest opportunity."

"I'm not sure of that," Evans said, tugging on his goatee reflectively. "But you seem to me to be the kind of young fellow who would prosper most anywhere."

"You're very kind to say that."

"I'm not at all kind . . . I am fair-minded, honest and very plain spoken. And, having said that, I'll also say that you don't seem like the kind of man that will be in law enforcement long . . . at least not as a lowly paid and poorly appreciated lawman."

"Who knows? Maybe I'll practice law again right here in Reno, if I tire of carrying a badge."

"That would be a wise thing to do. We have no quality in our local attorneys. Elbert Conroy is about the average, and you've seen how pathetic he is."

"Yes."

"So you would stand head and shoulders above your competition. Probably even replace me some day on the bench, if you play your cards right."

"That would be a *great* honor."

"Yes," the judge said, "however, something tells me that you aspire to even more. But we shall see." Judge Evans extended his bony hand. "I'll tell that little weasel Conroy that he needs to find another law office to rent and make sure the city gives him back his first month's rent."

"Thank you."

"You're welcome. And I'll see you this evening promptly at seven. You know, you should never keep a judge waiting."

"Believe me, I wouldn't dare do such a thing."

The judge tugged on his goatee again, and his eyes probed for a moment before he said, "I think you and I are going to get along very well, Marshal Peacock. Very well indeed."

"So do I."

"By the way, someone told me that Marshal Custis Long exited the train with you."

"That's right."

"Terrific lawman. None better to be found, and I'm sure that he was sent to . . . well, help you get accustomed to our Western ways and to facilitate your taking office."

"That, and helping me find out who killed Marshal Walker."

"Yes, terrible thing, that. Marshal Long is honest, tough and smart. We've come to trust and appreciate his work. He will be an excellent mentor and friend."

"I'm sure he will be."

"Good day," the judge said, grinning around his smoking cigar as he limped out the door.

When the judge was gone, Peacock went back to his desk with a smile on his face. Old Judge Evans would tell him everything he wanted to know tonight over dinner, wine and brandy. All about the town, the men of Reno who stood to gain the most from getting rid of Deke Walker . . . everything that was important. Furthermore, he'd be of enormous help when it came time to bring to justice whoever killed the United States marshal. And he'd also turn the other way if extreme measures had to be taken in order to clean up this town.

Yes sir, the judge was going to be of enormous help in getting off on the right foot . . . starting bright and early tomorrow . . . with or without Custis Long.

Chapter 10

On that first evening in Reno, Longarm had ordered his clothes to be cleaned and pressed, taken a bath, shaved and made himself quite presentable. Because he had visited so frequently over the past few years, he knew that he'd be recognized by friends ... and those not so friendly. And because he did have enemies, Longarm made sure that his firearms were loaded and in good working order. His side arm was a double-action Colt Model T .44-.40 caliber that he wore on his left hip, butt forward so that he could draw the weapon across his waist. He'd always worn his gun that way, and it suited him very well. His hideout gun was a .44 caliber derringer, so that his bullets were interchangeable between the two weapons. The derringer was cleverly fixed to a gold watch chain, whose opposite end was attached to a handsome Ingersol railroad watch. The small but powerful little derringer had saved his life on more occasions than he wished to remember.

The last item he put on before going out was his snuff brown Stetson with its flat crown. There was a mirror in his room, and he paused for a moment to study his reflection as he smoothed his handlebar mustache. He wasn't as handsome as Rutherford, but he thought he looked like a man who ought not to be trifled with and who had some grit.

I wonder if I'll see Dolly, he thought as he closed the door and went out through the small but respectable hotel and then headed for the center of town where he would eat.

"Evening, Marshal Long," someone called as he approached Virginia Street.

Custis turned to see a very short teenager who couldn't have stood over five feet four inches and whose name he'd forgotten. "Evening."

"You just get into town?"

"That's right."

"Staying long?"

"Depends."

"On what?"

Longarm couldn't help but smile. "At least partly on if you keep asking me so many questions."

"Geez," the kid said, "I guess I am being kinda nosy. Sorry about that. I was just hoping that I could buy you a cup of coffee or somethin' before you left town again. If you'll recall, you saved my father's life last year. His name was Joshua and mine is Jeremy. Jeremy Tuttle."

"Of course," Longarm said as if he'd known the name all along. "But you don't have to repay me anything. Your father is a good man and, if I remember correctly, your mother is a fine schoolteacher."

"That's right. And since meeting and watching you in action, I'd like to be a federal marshal some day. That's why I hoped we could talk. Maybe you could even give me some tips about how to draw fast and shoot straight."

"Maybe."

"How come you wear your gun with its butt forward?"

"It just suits me better," Longarm replied. "And when I'm seated, it's a whole lot easier and quicker to reach across my waist than to try and lift upward."

"Did you practice drawing and firing a lot when you were my age?"

"I was shooting rifles and pistols when I was barely old enough to walk."

"Are you as fast as Wyatt Earp or Wild Bill Hickock?"

"I don't know," Longarm said with a shrug of his broad shoulders. "I have never practiced for speed. What's most important is who shoots straight rather than who shoots first. A lot of times, some fella will open fire before me, but they're nearly always so excited and reckless that they miss."

The kid had sandy hair and large, inquisitive blue eyes. "But wouldn't you say it's best to shoot both straight *and* fast?"

"There's no denying that," Longarm replied as he started walking again.

"Where are you going now?"

"To eat."

"I'll buy," Jeremy offered.

"Nope. A federal officer is not supposed to take bribes of any kind."

"I ain't bribin' you!"

"Seems to me you're after information," Longarm said with mock seriousness. "And willing to buy my meal to get it. The only thing for me to do is to buy your dinner instead."

It was Jeremy's turn to grin. "Really?"

"Sure," Longarm told the kid. "That way it's all on the up-and-up."

"Well thanks aplenty!"

Longarm took Jeremy to the Pine Cone Cafe, one of the best little eateries in town. They had roast beef, potatoes, corn bread and coffee with apple pie for dessert. During the entire meal, Jeremy kept asking Longarm questions about how to be a gunfighter and how to kill a man before he killed you.

Finally, Longarm decided it was time to bring the kid back to reality. "This thing about shooting a man isn't all that you seem to think. There's nothing good about taking someone's life. It's about the worst thing one man can do to another."

"But some men deserve to die for their crimes, don't they?"

"Yes, they do. But my job is to take them alive and see that they get a trial by a proper judge and jury. That way, I don't have their deaths on my conscience. I'm just doing my part of the job and letting the court do theirs. Whatever they decide is usually just."

"Have you ever taken a man in who was sentenced to die but, deep down in your soul, you were sure that he was innocent?"

"I'm afraid that I have," Longarm told the kid. "There was a boy named Paul Stoner, about your age in Kansas, who killed his father . . . he actually blew his head clean off with a ten-gauge shotgun."

"His own father?"

"That's right. But the man was a drunk and he liked to beat up on the kid and his little brother."

"Then why would any jury sentence Paul to die?"

"Because he also killed his mother."

Jeremy's jaw dropped. "Young Paul Stoner shot both of his parents to death?"

"Yep."

"Then he *did* deserve to die."

"I don't think so," Longarm said quietly. "You see, for years Paul had been beaten so often and badly by his father that he wasn't right in the head anymore. And, to my way of thinking, his mother ought to have tried to protect him and his brother when he was young and helpless. But she didn't lift a finger to keep her sons safe."

"Yeah," Jeremy said slowly. "I see what you mean. But I still don't think Paul should have killed his own mother."

"It's true that he did wrong. But there were circumstances that I thought should have earned Paul Stoner a prison sentence instead of a hanging. You have to remember, Jeremy, that events in this world aren't always simply black or white, right or wrong. There are lots of grays and things that aren't so easy to figure out. That's why I have so much respect for a good judge."

"Did you feel bad arresting Stoner?"

"I did. He talked funny, and sometimes he'd have fits where he'd spit and choke. Like I said, Paul wasn't right in the head, but I never felt that he was mean."

"Only dangerous."

Longarm nodded. "That was a hard one for me. Most times, though, it's pretty obvious when someone needs to be either hanged or thrown in prison for a long, long time."

"Yeah, it must be a dangerous but exciting job."

"Sometimes. But a lot of the time, you're in a town where you don't yet know the people and what is really going on under the surface. Everyone smiles and acts nice when I'm around, but when I turn my back, bad things can happen."

"You mean like when they ambushed Deke Walker?"

"That's right." Longarm frowned. "Why did you say *they*?"

"Because I've thought a good deal about that killing, and I'm quite sure that more than one person was in on the murder."

"Care to explain further?"

"Sure," Jeremy said, leaning across the table and lowering his voice so that he could not be overheard. "I think that a couple of the local saloon owners got together and hired someone to put a bullet in Marshal Walker's back."

"Which saloon owners?"

"I can't say it was them for sure," Jeremy told him. "It's just a guess."

"Spit it out."

"Well, Mr. Abe Quarry owns the Palomino Saloon up in Virginia City and he also owns the Palomino House here in Reno."

"Yeah, I know that. So what?"

"Deke Walker was on Mr. Quarry a lot for getting his customers drunk and then rolling them in the alley behind his saloons. I heard the marshal get real mad and warn Mr. Quarry that the next time he found some poor cowboy or railroad worker knocked half silly in the back of the Palomino, the marshal would pitch Mr. Quarry in jail and throw away the key."

"Marshal Walker said that?"

Jeremy nodded his head. "And that ain't all. They had words. Mr. Quarry told the marshal that his days were numbered, and that if he were smart, he'd get the hell out of town."

"Interesting. So who was the other saloon owner?"

"His name is Kelly. I don't know his last name, but he owns the Lumber Mill Saloon and most of his customers are loggers. It's a real tough place and has at least a killing a month."

"Why?"

"Kelly has some women that work upstairs." Jeremy blushed. "I think you can guess what they do."

"I can."

"Well, the marshal told Kelly that his girls were causing too much trouble. He said that the girls were getting Kelly's customers drunk and drugged on something and that the girls had to go away. Kelly said they were staying, and Marshal Walker said he'd see about that."

"How do you know this?"

"I got to be real good friends with Marshal Walker. I told him, just like I told you, that I wanted to wear a badge someday."

"And what did Marshal Walker say to that?"

"He said I'd be smarter if I did something that had a brighter future."

"Deke said that?"

"He sure did. And so I asked him why, if he felt like that, he didn't turn in his own badge and find a better job. And you know what he told me?"

"What?"

"The marshal said that he couldn't think of a thing else that held much interest to him and besides, he was good at being a lawman and it was important work. Is that how you feel about it?"

"That's pretty close to the mark," Longarm answered. "When a man is good at something and feels it's important, he can't ask for much more. I tell you, Jeremy, there are an awful lot of folks that just draw their pay and hate what they do. They're unhappy and never much good for themselves or anyone else."

"So that's more important than the work having no future?"

Longarm chuckled. "There's a future in being a lawman. I just haven't figured out what it is yet."

"Are you going to arrest Kelly and Mr. Quarry?"

"No. I'll talk to your new town marshal, and we'll both decide what to do next. I appreciate your telling me this, but we have to remember that Marshal Walker was a man who went strictly by the rules. He brooked no one any leeway when it came to crossing the line between legal and illegal."

"Are you the same way?"

"Yes."

"Will our new federal marshal also be like that?"

Longarm frowned. "Marshal Peacock is going to be a good lawman, but he might need a little getting used to. That's one of the reasons why I came along to help, in addition to the investigation of Marshal Walker's murder."

"If there is anything I can do to help either one of you, I'd sure be happy to do it," Jeremy said eagerly. "If you want, I could sort of hang around those saloons when I'm not working down at the feed store and maybe I could hear something else that would be valuable."

Longarm knew that the kid desperately wanted to help solve the death of his friend, and he also knew that Jeremy might be invaluable. And yet . . . yet there was something in him that said Jeremy was too overeager and therefore, might get himself into serious trouble. Even dead.

"Look," he began, laying his hand on Jeremy's shoulder. "You've already tipped me off about Kelly and Abe Quarry."

"Yeah, but . . ."

"What you could do is just keep your ear to the ground about anyone else that would have had a reason to kill Marshal Walker."

"Okay, but . . ."

"I'm going to be up in Virginia City because I know

that there were others up there besides Quarry who had reasons to want Marshal Walker dead."

"What kind of reasons?"

"We can talk about that some other time," Longarm said, spying a cowboy that worked for Dolly Reardon's father. "In the meantime, you just make sure that you stay out of trouble. We're going to need your help in the days to come and I don't want anything bad happening to you."

"I'll be real careful, Marshal Long. I swear that I will."

"Good," Longarm said. "Now, I've got to run along."

He got up from the table and went over to greet the cowboy whose name was Spider McGee. Spider was a bronc buster on the Circle R Ranch and a real good all-around hand.

"Hey, Spider," Longarm called, going up to greet the tall, thin cowboy. "How have you been lately?"

"I been fine. Broke a couple of ribs last month after piling off a buckskin. But I got back on and taught him his manners. He's turning into a pretty good cow pony."

"Glad to hear that. How is everyone out on the Circle R?"

"If you mean Miss Reardon, she's just fine," Spider said with a twinkle in his eyes. "Her pa ain't married her off to anyone rich as hisself yet."

"That's good."

"I don't think Miss Reardon ever quite got over you, Marshal."

Longarm frowned. "Now why would you say a thing like that?"

"She just hasn't been interested in any men lately. At least, not so I could tell. She spends a lot of time out riding by herself."

"Huh," Longarm mused. "Does she look all right?"

"She's prettier than ever and just as spunky. She doesn't mind giving orders, either."

"Is that right?"

"Sure is. You gonna try and see her?" Spider asked, his usual grin fading.

"I don't know. Maybe not. I mean, her father has made it real clear that he has better things in mind for his daughter."

"Yeah, I know. But her father don't own her like he owns a horse. I think she feels real bad over you, Marshal."

Longarm expelled a deep breath. "I've got a lot on my mind over Deke's murder. I can't allow myself to become distracted."

"I can understand that. When I climb on board a bronc, I sure can't be thinkin' of anything else."

"Yeah."

"Well, Marshal. Even though you don't care to see Miss Reardon, she will be in town tomorrow shopping. I know that because she's always in town on Wednesdays. She buys all the grub and whatever else we need."

"Is that a fact?"

"Yes, it is. She has a routine, like the rest of us. She'll be in that big mercantile up the street between ten and eleven. Then after lunch at the Dorsey Cafe, she's going to be going over to the saddle shop where they're making her a custom saddle. After that, she'll probably be . . ."

"I get the picture, Spider."

"Just thought you'd like to know where she's going to be come tomorrow morning at ten o'clock to eleven. Her father won't be in town and . . ."

"Thanks," Longarm said. "But I think it's hopeless."

"Love is never hopeless, Marshal. Sometimes pathetic, sometimes sad, but never hopeless."

"I'll remember that."

"Hope you do," Spider told him before he sort of waddled away on his long bowed legs.

Chapter 11

Longarm didn't sleep particularly well that night because the thought of Dolly Reardon just wouldn't shake loose of his mind. He'd enjoyed the company of a lot of women in his lifetime, most of them relatively young and pretty. But Dolly was more than pretty, she was smart, funny, wise and sexy. She was more woman than he'd ever known, and the very thought that he could, if he chose to, see her tomorrow, was haunting.

I won't do it, he told himself over and over that night. *I'll make sure that I'm somewhere else when she goes shopping. Maybe I'll even get up early and head up to the Comstock Lode.*

But, deep in his troubled heart, Longarm knew that he had to see Dolly and the sooner, the better. She was like a thirst that time and distance hadn't quenched. She was like a rose that would not wilt and whose beauty was impressed upon his mind.

Oh, he'd be there when she went into the mercantile at ten o'clock and nothing or no one could possibly stop him from seeing her. And once that happened, Longarm really wasn't sure what he would do or say. He might be struck dumb and look the fool, or words of love might pour from his lips.

He absolutely hadn't a clue.

Longarm was up with the sun and dressed in his finest by eight o'clock that morning. Too nervous to eat, he paid a long overdue visit to the barbershop for a haircut and shave. Then, still with time to kill, he went to the very mercantile where he expected to meet Dolly and bought himself a new shirt, tie and hat.

"Marshal you look smashing," the owner of the store exclaimed. "Shall I wrap up your purchases?"

"Nope, I'm wearing them out the door."

"Good. And what would you like me to do with your old hat, shirt and tie?"

"I don't care. Give them to someone who needs clothes or else throw them away."

Longarm paid for his new finery and went outside checking his pocket watch. It was only nine o'clock. Still an hour to kill before he could hope to see Dolly.

"Well there you are!" Peacock called as he came striding down the boardwalk. "I thought you'd come by the office, and we'd go for breakfast and coffee this morning."

"That'd be fine."

"You look a little tired. Didn't you sleep well?"

"Not too good," Longarm admitted.

"We have a lot of work cut out for ourselves. Are you leaving for the Comstock Lode this afternoon or staying around a few days to help me catch whoever killed Marshal Walker?"

"I haven't decided," Longarm told him. "Let's just take it a bit at a time. Breakfast sounds good."

"I'm buying."

"I figured as much."

114

As they started up the street toward a cafe, Peacock said, "I had a very interesting and, I think, valuable evening."

"That right?"

"Yes. I dined with Judge Evans. He's quite a fellow."

"That he is."

"Thinks very highly of you."

"Glad to hear that," Longarm replied. "The judge has my highest regard. He's a man of great integrity."

"I also met a kid named Jeremy Tuttle. He said that he knew and admired you."

"My, my," Longarm drawled. "I guess I'm an idol around these parts. A living legend."

"Sarcasm," Peacock said, "just doesn't become you and you should always avoid it. Do you want to hear what Jeremy had to say about who he thinks is behind Marshal Walker's death?"

"Of course."

"The kid overheard Walker and a man named Abe Quarry arguing," Peacock said. "Jeremy told me that he heard the marshal warning Quarry about rolling cowboys that he and his girls got drunk in the Palomino House as well as the Palomino Saloon up in Virginia City. Have you heard of Abe Quarry?"

"I'm afraid so."

"That bad, huh?"

"Let's just say that he would not do well back East in your high society. He's ruthless and a bad apple."

"Then he could be Walker's assassin."

"Yeah, but an argument isn't evidence of a murder."

"Jeremy also heard the marshal warn the owner of the Lumber Mill Saloon to stop doing the same crimes against drunken loggers. Do you know the owner?"

"I know of him," Longarm said. "His name is William

Kelly. If anything, he's even slimier than Abe Quarry."

"The kid says that Quarry and Kelly are in cahoots. A couple of crooked Irish micks. It seems to me that we might have already identified the murderers."

Longarm wasn't so sure and so he said, "I'll tell you something. I like Jeremy Tuttle. He's a good kid, but he has a lot of wild ideas about what it takes to become a lawman and about how a lawman operates. I tried to explain that the work is most often dull and repetitive. That there's little glory and way too little pay for the chances we take and the long hours we spend on investigations. But Jeremy never listened."

Peacock shrugged his broad shoulders. "So he's got this fantasy about becoming a marshal. Maybe you were just like him when you were young. I know that I was. By the time Jeremy is old enough to know better, he still might want to wear a badge."

"I hope you're right," Longarm replied. "But the point I was making is that the kid is so eager to be a part of our investigation that I think it's fairly likely that he'd jump to conclusions without a shred of evidence to back them up."

"All right. So what do we do?" Peacock said, looking impatient and unhappy. "Just forget about those tips?"

"Nope. I think we ought to pay a visit to Abe Quarry and William Kelly today."

"I agree! Let's go find them."

"No," Longarm said. "In the first place, they stay up all night in their saloons overseeing the help and their cash registers, so they won't even be awake until at least noon. And, in the second place, we need to have breakfast and then snoop around a bit more. Also, I have . . . well, some things I need to do this morning."

"What could be more important than this investigation?" Peacock demanded. "My gosh, I practically hand you the names of the killers and you act as if this information is of little or no value. Deke Walker was *your* friend, not mine. I thought you'd jump at this news, and now I don't understand how you can be so . . . so cavalier!"

"Rutherford, just calm down and buy me breakfast. Things move slower out in the West than they do in New York City. Quarry and Kelly aren't going anywhere, and if we get all excited and start asking them the tough questions now . . . before we have something more solid than what a kid overheard . . . then we'll mess up our investigation."

Longarm wasn't particularly hungry, but he made himself eat. He tried to listen to Peacock, but his mind was on Dolly and it must have showed because the newly appointed deputy finally asked, "What's the matter with you this morning? I don't think you've heard a word I've said."

"Sure I have," Longarm lied as he drained his coffee cup and then consulted his pocket watch to note that it was almost ten o'clock. "It's just that I have some things to do right now."

"Can I help you?"

"No."

"Then what am I supposed to do . . . just sit around on my hands and wait for you?"

"What you ought to do is to start making everyone's acquaintance. People need to know that you're the new lawman in their town. You've got a lot of charm . . . use it. Try to ingratiate yourself with the town's businessmen. They're going to want to know if you're here to find out who murdered Marshal Walker, and you tell them that

117

you've come to do that, but also to maintain law and order."

Peacock frowned. "You aren't planning to visit Quarry and Kelly without me, are you?"

"No."

"Because I wouldn't appreciate that one bit. I mean, I'm staying here in Reno, and I don't want to be upstaged, to put it quite bluntly."

"I wouldn't think of *upstaging* you," Longarm replied.

"All right then. I'll start walking around and greeting people. But I'd still like to know what you're going to do next."

"I'm going to meet an old . . . old friend."

"Someone who might be able to shed some light on the murder?"

"Maybe," Longarm said. "I don't know."

"Hmmm," Peacock mused. "You're acting sort of strange this morning and that has whet my curiosity."

"Apply your curiosity to our murder investigation . . . not to me," Longarm told him as he prepared to leave and head for the mercantile where Dolly was probably already shopping. "And thanks for the breakfast."

"You're welcome," Peacock said, as Longarm headed out the door.

It was five minutes past the hour when Longarm stepped into the mercantile and saw Dolly inspecting some canned goods. He could feel his heart quicken and when he walked up behind her and spoke, his voice sounded strained and unfamiliar.

"Hello there, Miss Reardon. Finding what you're looking for this morning?"

She stiffened and he heard her take a deep breath, then turn slowly on her heels and look up at his face. "As a matter of fact, I think I just found *exactly* what I've been looking for. Something I thought I'd lost."

"You didn't lose me," Longarm said, his voice husky with emotion. "I just went away for a while."

"Why? Why did you leave without even a good-bye? Without a word of explanation?"

"You know the reason."

"My father." It was a statement, not a question.

"Yes. And I doubt he's had a change of heart and is going to welcome me back in town."

"No," Dolly admitted, "Father hasn't had a change of heart, and he'll be absolutely furious when he discovers you are back and we're seeing each other."

"Are we seeing each other?" Longarm asked.

"Without a doubt or hesitation. Starting right now and for the rest of the day."

Longarm smiled and then bent his head. A tender kiss to start, then the old hunger took over and they strained in each other's embrace, lips hot and hungry. Breath coming fast.

"Holy Moses," Longarm breathed, pulling away and studying her lovely face. "I don't know what it is that you do to me, but it sure is powerful."

"It was that way between us from the start. Why do you suppose that is?"

"I don't know. Some kind of animal magnetism, I'd guess."

"Sounds good to me. Can you wait until I finish doing my shopping before we go to your room?"

He frowned. "Dolly, I'm not sure that would be such a great idea. You are a part of this town and county, I'm not. You're the one that would suffer the gossip, not me."

"I don't care what people say or think. Do you?"

"Not really," he told her. "But I don't want to see you get hurt."

"Are you leaving me again without a good-bye?"

He shook his head. "But nothing has changed. I couldn't be a cattle rancher. I still love what I do."

"Then maybe I'll have to marry you and live in Reno."

"You'd do that even knowing that I'd be gone and in danger weeks on end?"

"If that's the way it has to be," she said, "then I will."

"And what about your father?"

"He'll get over it."

"He'll disinherit you."

"I don't care. Do you?"

"Hell no! I don't give a damn for his money."

"Neither do I. So why don't you go busy yourself looking at saddles or something while I finish my ranch shopping. When that's done, we can go find a place to be alone together."

"All right," he agreed. "Just as long as . . ."

Dolly's finger pressed firm against his lips silencing them. "Custis, I love your southern chivalry. The way you can't stand the idea of damaging a lady's reputation. But there's just one problem."

"What's that?"

"I'm not a lady. Never have been and never will be. I'm a woman who is madly in love with the handsomest federal marshal ever to pin on a badge."

"I don't pin it on very often. I usually carry it in my vest pocket."

She giggled. "I know that, silly."

"And after you see the town's new federal marshal, you're probably going to think that I'm only the second handsomest lawman you've ever seen."

"Is that right?"

"Afraid so. He's an Easterner from New York City. Rich, handsome and a well-educated attorney."

"So why is he here in Reno?"

"He has the same romantic notion of a Western lawman as Jeremy Tuttle."

"Is he honest?"

"I don't know. I guess we'll soon find out. I do know that he's very ambitious. He won't be content to be a lowly paid lawman for long unless I badly miss my guess."

Dolly pursed her lips. "Sounds interesting. When do I get to meet him?"

"Never, if I had my druthers."

She smiled. "Don't tell me that you're jealous."

"Not yet, but I could be."

"What is his name?"

"Rutherford Peacock. And he *is* sort of like a peacock."

"Well," she said, kissing Longarm on the cheek and giving him a gentle shove. "I will meet your peacock but you don't have anything to worry about. You're my man . . . so long as you behave yourself and don't ever leave me guessing again."

"I promise I'll never do that a second time."

She threw herself into his arms and hugged his neck tightly. "That's all that I need to ever hear, Custis. Now let me try to gather my wits and finish the ranch shopping."

"I'll be waiting outside."

"I'll be with you soon," she promised.

Longarm headed up the aisle feeling as if he were walking on air. But the moment he reached the front of the store, there was Peacock with a curious look on his face. "So now I know what had you so distracted over breakfast this morning."

It was all that Longarm could do to be civil. "Why aren't you doing something productive?"

"I am! You told me to go meet the businessmen and that's what I've been doing. I'm here to meet the fellow that owns this store."

"Get lost."

Peacock chuckled and gazed down the dimly lit aisle toward Dolly Reardon. "Aren't you even going to introduce me to this woman that has made you so giddy?"

"Dammit, I'm not *giddy* and I've no intention of introducing you to her."

"Then I'll just have to introduce myself."

Rutherford started to push by Longarm in the narrow aisle but was stopped in his tracks by the grip on his arm. "What are you doing?"

"She's busy shopping, and you're leaving her alone!"

"You engaged or secretly married?"

"No."

Peacock shrugged as if he did not understand. "Then have the laws of the United States changed so that a man can *own* a woman? Has slavery been reinstated?"

"Back off, turn around and head for the door," Longarm said. "I'll be right behind you, and we're going to have a little man-to-man talk."

"Fine. I can hardly wait."

"Neither can I," Longarm gritted as he spun Peacock around and shoved him up the aisle.

Chapter 12

"All right, what's the problem?" Peacock said, pivoting about when they had reached the street.

Longarm had no intention of discussing his love life or any other part of his life in front of strangers. He spied an opening between the mercantile and the next business and said, "Follow me."

Longarm marched down the corridor until he reached the back alley and then he turned around and confronted the young marshal. "I'm just going to tell you this once," he said through gritted teeth. "I am in love with the woman you saw in there, and I want you to leave her the hell alone. Is that understood?"

"In love?" Peacock echoed with a wicked grin on his lips. "My, my. And I thought you were the dedicated bachelor. The man with a heart of stone. The epitome of the lonely warrior of the West."

"I'm not going to bandy words with you. Just don't mess around with Miss Reardon."

His eyebrows shot up. "Are you . . . engaged to be married?"

"No."

"I see." Peacock tapped his forefinger against his perfect teeth as if examining some great mystery. "Then you're just . . . lovers?"

Longarm's fist lashed out and connected solidly on the point of Peacock's chin, knocking him sprawling to the ground. The Easterner shook his head as if to clear away the cobwebs, then slowly pushed himself to his feet, brushing dust off his clothing. "Damn you, Custis, you had no reason to do that."

"I had *every* reason. I'm sick and tired of your smart alecky attitude. I don't like being taunted, and I won't stand for it even a little."

The man rubbed his jaw and glared at Longarm. "I ought to whip you."

"Go ahead and try," Longarm growled.

But Peacock took a deep breath and, after a long pause, said, "No, because that's exactly what you want."

"What is that supposed to mean?"

"I'd whip you, of that I have no doubt," Peacock said. "But I wouldn't come out unscathed. And then you'd use your popularity to bad-mouth me and ruin any chance I have of finding Walker's murderer."

"You're crazy! What goes on here and now has nothing to do with our work. So quit trying to make excuses and let's get after it. I'm fed up with your sarcasm and arrogance."

"I'm not the one that's arrogant . . . *you* are!"

Longarm stepped forward and drove a straight right hand at Peacock's mouth. But the man slipped the punch and countered with a hard right cross that caught Longarm high on the cheekbone and rocked him back on his heels.

"I don't want to do this now," Peacock said as he and Longarm began to circle each other. "If we come out of this alley all bloodied up, how is that going to look? The people here expect us to uphold the law, not be brawling in some dirty back alley. A hard fight will make *both* of us look bad. We're going to need to work together if we have any chance of getting Deke Walker's murderer."

Longarm knew that Rutherford was right, but his blood was boiling, and what he really wanted to do was to mess up that handsome, aristocratic face.

"I'll leave your girlfriend alone," Peacock offered. "Though it galls me no end to be told who I can or cannot spark."

"I don't believe a word you say."

"I will! I've already found a woman or two here in Reno. I need your help a lot more than I need another woman to worry about, and you ought to know that's the gospel truth."

"You wouldn't get anywhere with Dolly even if she wasn't my girl," Longarm said. "She'd see right through you and laugh."

"If you're so certain of that," Peacock said, "why are you acting like such a lovesick and crazy fool?"

Longarm knew he was overreacting to the thought of Peacock trying to steal Dolly away from him. He wasn't normally a bit jealous, and he didn't like the way it felt right now.

"Okay," he grated, touching his cheekbone to see if there was any blood. There wasn't, but he knew that there'd be swelling and a dark bruise where the man's fist had landed so expertly.

"Maybe," Peacock said, "when this is all over, we can be friends. Or, on the other hand, perhaps we can find out who the best man really is."

"It's me," Longarm said without hesitation. "You're a man with a closet full of skeletons. A fella who couldn't cut it for whatever reason in New York City, so you de-

125

cided you'd come out here and make your name and reputation among the country folk. The uneducated and unwashed people of the West that you consider so inferior to yourself."

"You got it all wrong."

"Have I?" Longarm started to leave the man. "We'll find out soon enough."

"When are we going to go talk to Quarry and Kelly?" Peacock shouted after him. "Or has your lady love completely taken over your mind?"

Longarm ignored the insult. "I'll see you at your office around five o'clock. Then we'll go see Quarry and Kelly."

"I'll be there."

"You'd better be," Longarm warned as he headed back toward the front of the street.

They had found a secret place a half mile stroll up the Truckee River where they could be intimate and undisturbed in a small dell surrounded by cottonwoods and thickets. Longarm and Dolly lay on the grass beside the rushing water and gazed up at the sky.

Dolly asked, "Please be honest, Custis."

"Always."

"If it wasn't for Deke being murdered and the fact that you've got a young, opportunistic deputy marshal that you can't stand and don't trust, would you have ever come back to Reno to claim my hand in marriage?"

He wanted to say yes, but instead was completely honest and replied, "I don't know."

"Did you see other women since we were together?"

This was going to be hard. Very hard. "Yes, I'm afraid that I did see a woman or two since we parted."

"But I never laid with any other men! Not once, and I sure had plenty of chances." Her voice shook with hurt

126

and anger. "Custis, you know that I had lots of chances, don't you?"

"Sure you did."

"Then why weren't you true to me?"

Suddenly, Longarm was wishing he was someplace else. Most anyplace else, in fact. "Dolly, I didn't think we'd ever see each other again. That our time was past. My heart was nearly broken, but I figured you were better off without me."

"Well, dammit, you figured wrong!"

"But you love your father and that ranch."

"Yes, but I love you even more."

"Are you sure that in six months or six years you wouldn't regret marrying me?" Longarm asked.

"I'm completely sure."

"All right then," he said. "We'll be married."

She brightened. "When?"

"When we go back to Denver. After this case is over, and I can leave Reno with a clear conscience."

"You mean when you've gotten Deke's killer, and you've either run off or come to peace with Rutherford Peacock?"

"That's about the size of it."

Dolly rolled over to gaze down at this face. "You're going to have a shiner. He really socked you a good one."

"Not as good as I socked him."

"What did you fight over?"

Longarm was embarrassed to tell her the truth but he did it anyway. "I told him to leave you alone."

"You told him that?" she asked, looking amused and pleased.

"Yeah."

"Well, I suppose that you could have told him that and avoided a fight."

127

"Maybe."

The amusement slipped away to be replaced by a look of concern. "Custis, you *do* trust me, don't you?"

"Sure."

"Then why the warning?"

"Look. Can't we find something else to talk about?"

"You were worried that I might . . . might fall for this man?" she asked in amazement.

"No. Yes. Rutherford Peacock, he's the kind of man that attracts women like honey does to bees."

"Custis, I can't imagine that you've never noticed that you also attract women like bees to honey."

"I'm not so sure of that," he told her. "But I can say that I've never seen anyone like Rutherford who has the power to make women act so foolish and giddy. Grown women. Old women. He makes them act like schoolgirls."

"He sounds . . . intriguing."

"He's flawed, but I can't tell you exactly why or how. I'd just like you to be forewarned that the man is not what he seems."

Dolly kissed his lips and ran her tongue over them so provocatively that Longarm felt himself grow large in his pants. "If Rutherford Peacock is so flawed and unworthy, why would your boss send him out here as a federal marshal?"

Longarm chose his words carefully. "Because this town has never been able to keep an honest town marshal. One who will uphold the law. And also because Rutherford has powerful friends in Washington, D.C., and managed to get the appointment. There may even be other reasons that I don't know of, but that is enough."

"All right," she said, kissing him again. "Let's talk about us."

"No," Longarm said, pushing up her riding skirt and

running his hand up her smooth thigh. "Let's not talk about anything. Let's just make passionate love."

"Right here by the river?"

"Why not? The river doesn't care. It won't blush and turn pink."

"Yes, but there are people who walk along this bank fishing. This is also a favorite place for other lovers who like to take a quiet stroll and steal secret kisses."

"Then we'll show them there are better things for lovers to do than to stroll and just kiss," he said, voice growing husky with passion as he pushed her skirt up higher and began to remove her petticoats and underclothes.

"Custis, please stop," she begged, clutching him ever tighter, "we might be seen!"

"I've been waiting too long to worry about that now. Believe me, this won't take long!"

It only took a moment or two for them to join. Longarm plunged deeply into Dolly, and she cried out with pleasure. The old magic they remembered as being so special hadn't diminished in the least since the last time they'd had a wild romp in a haystack out behind a livery. And now, as Longarm drove himself deeper and faster into the woman he loved, he felt as if the top of his head was going to blow off as Dolly began to cry out in her own rapturous passion.

"Oh, Custis! Oh, my . . . oh, oh! Don't stop! Never stop!"

Longarm didn't want to ever stop but he was so excited that he took her in a thundering rush, pumping great torrents of his hot seed into her straining body. Dolly shuddered and screamed as her own soaring and explosive climax took her like a Texas tornado.

Their bodies were like a runaway train, and they kept

129

slamming into each other long after they were both spent and gasping.

"Oh, Custis," she sobbed, "you can't imagine how I dreamed of this moment. How I ached every night for this sweet release."

"Me, too."

She stiffened ever so slightly. "But you admitted that you had other women." She sobbed and her eyes grew misty with tears. "Custis, I still can't believe you'd do that!"

"Dolly, I'm sorry. I was weak of the flesh. But none of those other women meant anything to me."

"Are you sure?"

"Yep."

"Because I couldn't stand it if you were seeing anyone else. It would tear my heart out. It would feel like it was hurled to the ground and run over by stampeding cattle."

"I won't ever cheat on you, Dolly."

"Do I have your *solemn* word?"

"You do." Longarm meant every word when he vowed, "You'll be my wedded wife, and I will be faithful until the day that I die."

Dolly clutched him tightly and warm tears flowed down her rosy cheeks. She was about to say something, but then they both heard the crack of a branch and looked sideways to see a teenage couple staring at them with their mouths hanging open and their eyes bulging half out of their pimply faces.

"Oh, no," Dolly groaned, turning her face away. "I can't believe it's Arnie and Hannah! Oh gawd, no!"

"Get out of here!" Longarm shouted, waving his arms and feeling almost as terrible as Dolly. "Go . . . go fishing or something!"

The young couple grabbed each other's hands and went flying off into the thickets.

"Look," Longarm said, "they're probably doing it themselves, but never realized it could get so wild. I wouldn't worry about . . ."

"I *know* them!" Dolly cried, pushing him off of her and then pulling up her undergarments. "Arnie's father owns the saddle shop where my father buys all of his leather goods. And Hannah's father is our banker! He knows everyone in this town, and he couldn't keep a secret if his life depended upon it. Oh my gawd, this is a disaster!"

Longarm could see that she was extremely upset. He helped Dolly to her feet and even brushed the dead grass off her skirt and blouse. "I should have listened to you," he admitted. "I should have found us a room someplace or . . . or even taken you back to that haystack."

"I don't believe this," Dolly moaned, looking as if she were going to puke. "Before morning, what was seen here will be described in great and gleeful detail all over town, and you can just bet that it will somehow reach my father."

"Look. I could run after them and . . ."

"And then what?" Dolly turned on him, eyes bright with anger and unspoken accusations. "Arrest those kids for happening to come upon a couple yelling their heads off and locked in a passionate embrace?"

Longarm could see that she had a point, but he persisted. "I . . . I could scare them bad enough that they'd never dare utter of word of what they saw us doing."

"No. It's too late for that. And besides, they're probably almost to Virginia Street by now."

"Then what happens next?"

"I'm going to have to tell my father about us tonight when I get back to the ranch."

"I'll go with you."

"No!" She lowered her voice. "You know that he'll go crazy. Crazy enough to grab a shotgun and try to blow your pants off and everything in them."

Longarm expected that was true. "All right. Then you tell him that I'm coming to take you away as soon as I've caught or killed Deke Walker's murderer. Tell him that I won't be run off, threatened or made to feel unworthy. You tell him he can either have a son-in-law or he can lose his daughter. He can't have it both ways anymore."

"All right, that's what I'll tell Father."

"He won't lay a hand on you, will he?" Longarm's jaw clenched. "Because, if I thought he might, I'd never let you go back to the ranch without being at your side."

"Father has never hit me, and he won't start now," she promised. "I'll stand right up to him and tell him that we're in love. I'll tell him that just because my mother ran off with another man shortly after I was born that it doesn't mean a couple can't be married and live happily together for the rest of their natural lives."

"You tell him that," Longarm said, buttoning up his pants and reaching for his gunbelt. "You tell him that I'm a good man, but that I just can't be a cattle rancher, and I won't give up my profession. At least not yet."

"But someday, maybe when we have children."

"Maybe so."

Dolly straightened her hair and gave him a quick kiss on the lips. "I'd better go back into town alone."

"What difference does it make if everyone will hear what we just did here beside the river?"

"Well, some people might not hear it," she replied as she turned to leave.

"Dolly!"

She stopped and looked back. "Yes?"

132

"When will I see you again?"

She raised her chin proudly. "Make it when we are leaving for Denver to be married. Just get what you have to do done here, Custis, and then come out and take me away."

"All right. I will. I'll take care of business, and then I'll take care of you."

"I know, darling. Good-bye!"

Longarm stood by the river and watched her disappear into the thickets just like the two damn teenagers who'd watched them in their most intimate embrace.

"Damn," he whispered, reaching down for his hat. "This day just isn't starting off so good. No, sir, not good at all."

Chapter 13

Peacock was ready and waiting when Longarm showed up at his office that afternoon at five o'clock. He was also clutching a shotgun in his big hands and looked as if he might decide to use it on Longarm.

"What's that for?" Longarm demanded.

"I expect that we might have some trouble with this pair when we confront them."

"Put the shotgun away," Longarm ordered. "We're just going to talk to Quarry and Kelly to see what we can find out. Maybe we'll get lucky, and they'll have a slip of the tongue, although that's unlikely."

"Dammit, Custis, if I am carrying that double-barreled shotgun, they'd be more likely to talk!"

But Longarm disagreed. "That's not at all true. Abe Quarry didn't get where he is today by being easily frightened. Quite the opposite. And as for Kelly, well, he's probably even tougher."

"All right," Peacock said, reluctantly putting the shotgun down and patting his side arm. "Let's stop talking and get busy."

That was just fine with Longarm, who headed out the

door. He didn't say a word until they entered the Palomino House. It was dim inside, and there were only a half dozen cowboys sipping whiskey and beer when the bartender came over to ask what they wanted to drink. "Can I help—Oh, it's you, Marshal Long. What are you doing in here?"

"I'm looking for your boss."

"He's unavailable," the bartender snapped. "Maybe you'd like to leave and go find another place to drink."

Peacock's hand shot across the bar top. Almost quicker than the eye, he grabbed the insolent man by the shirtfront and slammed his face down hard against the bar. Then, he raised his head and stared at his broken and bleeding nose. "I don't think you have enough respect for the law. My name is Marshal Rutherford Peacock, and I'm going to insist that you learn some manners. Now tell your boss to get out here and to do it fast or I'll come looking for him and when we meet, I'll break his nose just like I just broke yours!"

The bartender's eyes were glassy, and it was clear that he was in agony. He cupped his face with both hands. Blood trickled down both wrists, ruining the starched white cuffs of his fancy silk shirt.

Rearing back, he cried, "Gawd damn you! You broke my nose and I swear that I'll . . ."

Whatever the man was about to swear was forgotten as Peacock drew his six-gun, cocked it and aimed it at the bartender's bloody face. "Move!"

The man's nerve broke, and he ran for the back room.

"How'd I do?" Rutherford asked, holstering his gun as the small but tough crowd of loggers stared at them with ill-concealed dislike.

"You did just fine," Longarm said approvingly. "I was just about to teach that man some manners myself."

"What can we expect from Quarry?" Rutherford whispered so that he couldn't be overheard.

"I don't know him well enough to even guess." Longarm heard shouts from the back room, then the door burst open and the notorious Irish saloon owner shouted, "All right! Which one of you broke Carl's gawd damn nose?"

"I did," Peacock said, reaching across the bar for a bottle of whiskey and a couple of glasses. "You need to teach your hired help better manners."

Quarry was a bull with thick shoulders so hunched with muscle that it seemed as if he had no neck. He wasn't tall. Perhaps five foot ten inches, but he weighed well over two hundred pounds. His face had probably once been handsome, but that was when he'd been in his prime and before his nose had been fist-busted on several occasions and someone had carved up the left side of his face from his brow to his jawline with a knife or a broken whiskey bottle.

"You son of a bitch!" Quarry raged. "If you weren't wearing that badge, I'd rearrange that face of yours so that it looked like the ass end of a mule!"

"Oh?" Rutherford started to unpin his badge but Longarm grabbed his arm and said, "Maybe we've gotten off to a bad start here, Mr. Quarry. Why don't we all have a drink and calm down? We just came in to introduce ourselves and have a friendly conversation."

"I got nothing to say to either one of you!"

"In that case," Longarm said, drawing his own six-gun, "I'm afraid that we'll have to arrest you and put you in jail."

The Irishman's round, scarred face turned purple with fury. "For what?"

"I'll think of something. Now, do you want to cooperate and do this the easy way? Or do we have to take

137

you off to jail? And then who would watch over your bar? Your bartender isn't coming back, and I expect that these boys here might not be above taking advantage of the situation and helping themselves to some free liquor."

Quarry could obviously see that as a real possibility because he visibly regained control over himself and grated, "All right. Grab three glasses and let's get this over with."

"Good thinking," Peacock told the man.

When they took their seats in the most remote part of the dirty saloon, whose sawdusted floors should have been replaced years earlier, Longarm got right to the point. "We think you can help us find out who killed Marshal Deke Walker."

Quarry scoffed and tossed down his whiskey. "You're crazy! I don't know a thing about that bloody business."

"Is that right?" Longarm leaned back in his chair and gave the man a faintly contemptuous look. "That's not what we're hearing."

Quarry's confident smile slipped. "What is it that you're hearing then?"

"We've been told that you shot Marshal Walker to death."

"*Who* told you?"

"We're not going to say because we think you'd also have them killed."

"Ha!" Quarry roared. "You boys been drinkin' before you came here? 'Cause, if you're sober, you're a couple of fools if you think I ambushed Deke Walker. I'm a terrible shot!"

"Then you hired someone to do it," Peacock said, managing his own relaxed smile. "But either way, the word is out that you're behind the murder, and we're going to get some evidence that will put you in prison for life . . .

or maybe even put your neck in a hangman's noose. Abe, we *know* you're the man responsible for that murder. One way or the other, we'll get the evidence we need to make the case."

"I think you boys are bluffin'."

They *were* bluffing, but Longarm had found that sometimes it was the only way to make a suspect lose his composure and blurt something vital to a difficult investigation. "We have a witness that says you threatened to kill Marshal Walker."

"Then he's a liar! I never threatened the marshal."

"Our witness is ready to make a sworn testimony before Judge Evans."

"Who is he? Show me this witness."

But Longarm shook his head. "We're not stupid. If you had Marshal Walker murdered, you'd do the same to our witness."

Quarry poured himself another whiskey. His eyes narrowed and he studied Longarm, then Peacock, before he lowered his voice and said, "All right. You want to know the truth?"

"Sure!" Peacock exclaimed, favoring Longarm with a look of triumph.

"I think you're both full of horseshit up to your ears."

Longarm had seen it coming, but Peacock was caught off guard and now he was furious. "Custis, let's take him to jail, and I'll throw away the key."

"You've got no right to do that!" Quarry bellowed, pushing out of his chair.

"Sit down," Longarm ordered. "We aren't finished with this conversation."

Quarry took his seat. His eyes narrowed and he lowered his voice. "Do you really want know who stood the most to have Deke Walker murdered?"

"We're listening," Peacock said.

"The one you need to take a hard look at is our local cattle baron, Miles Reardon."

Longarm tried not to show surprise. "Why?"

"Because Deke was after his daughter."

If he hadn't been sitting in a chair, Longarm would have been rocked back on his heels. "I don't believe that."

"That's because you can't admit that your friend Deke Walker was after *your* woman!" the saloon owner crowed, jabbing a thick finger at Longarm. "And you thought he was nothing more than a simple lawman. Well, you couldn't have been more mistaken. Walker wanted to marry into that ranching family in the worst way. And of course, the high and mighty Miles Reardon was outraged."

"I don't believe a word you're saying," Longarm snapped, barely able to keep from punching the saloon owner.

"Hold on a minute, Custis!" Peacock exclaimed. "This man isn't finished, and I'd like to hear what else he has to say about the Reardon family."

"I don't," Longarm said, coming to his feet.

"Take it easy," Quarry said. "It's no secret that you and Reardon's daughter had a thing going, but neither is it a secret that Deke Walker had set his sights on that girl and her father's cattle ranch. If you don't believe me, just ask around. I'm telling you the truth when I say that Miles Reardon hated Deke Walker and considered the man a real threat to his daughter. If I were you, I'd follow that lead."

"We will," Peacock promised. "But we understand that Kelly over at the Lumber Mill Saloon is also involved. Do you think that he was the one that had Marshal Walker shot in ambush?"

"William Kelly? Hell, no!" Quarry barked. "Kelly is a successful businessman just like myself. Why would he get himself into a mess like that?"

"For money," Longarm surprised himself by saying. "Reardon might have paid him to kill the marshal."

Quarry shook his head. "Not a chance! Kelly would have laughed Reardon out of his saloon. I'm telling you both that if you really want to find out who murdered your old friend Deke Walker, then the place to start is the Reardon Ranch because that old man hired someone to ambush the marshal in order to keep him away from his daughter."

"I can't believe that Dolly would have given Deke Walker the time of day," Longarm muttered.

"Maybe not, but he was hot for her. And besides, who knows what she was up to when no one was looking? Marshal Long, I know you're sweet on her, but sometimes the loveliest roses have the sharpest thorns."

"Let's go see Kelly," Peacock told Longarm. "This man isn't going anywhere if we need to talk to him again."

The Irishman came to his feet now that he knew he wasn't going to jail and said, "I don't appreciate the way you came charging into my saloon and busting up my bartender's nose."

"It doesn't matter what you appreciate," Longarm told the man. "We have a job to do."

"Then start with Miles Reardon! Or are you too blinded by love to see the truth?"

Longarm went outside and found a cheroot in his coat pocket. He used his teeth to rip off its tip and then he spat it into the street and struck a match so hard that it flared and died.

"Here," Peacock said, lighting the cheroot for him and then removing a good cigar from his coat pocket. "I know

141

this is hard to accept, but there is the possibility that Quarry is telling the truth and Reardon had Deke ambushed."

Longarm shook his head. "I don't believe it."

"Perhaps that's because you're too emotionally involved with Miss Reardon. But I'm not, and I need to at least consider the possibility. Did your late friend ever show any . . . interest in Miss Reardon?"

"Look," Longarm said, "the idea that Deke was in love with Miss Reardon is preposterous."

"Then he didn't like women?"

"I didn't say that."

"Then why is it so preposterous? Haven't you ever heard the fairy tale of the frog who dreamed of becoming a prince and marrying the princess?"

"As a matter of fact I haven't."

"That fairy tale demonstrates that anyone can dream of being the chosen one by a lovely, lovely woman no matter how low their status in life or how physically unattractive." Peacock frowned. "Describe Deke Walker."

"Why?" Longarm asked.

"About how old was the man?"

"Thirty. Maybe thirty-five."

"Tall? Short? Skinny or fat?"

"About average height. Around five nine or five ten. He was slender."

"Did our late marshal ever visit the ladies upstairs at the Palomino House?"

Longarm was getting annoyed. He didn't want to talk or even think about Deke's shortcomings. "I don't know. I never asked him about his personal business."

"Did he have a girlfriend?" Peacock asked. "Had he been married before? I'd like to know how the marshal responded to beautiful women."

"Look," Longarm said, trying his best to be patient. "Deke Walker was an outstanding marshal. We were friends, but he wasn't the kind of man who shared his personal life. Deke was a loner, and he pretty much devoted all his energy to upholding the law here in Reno. He had a big job, and one that I doubt you can handle."

"That remains to be seen," Peacock said. "But right now we are talking about Deke Walker, not me. How ambitious was the man?"

"As far as I knew," Longarm said, "he didn't want to do anything more than be a big town marshal."

"You're too close to both Deke and Miss Reardon to be objective."

"Not true," Longarm shot back. "It's just that I know them both well enough to say that they could never have fallen in love or had any romantic interest in each other."

"We'll see," Peacock replied. "But what Abe Quarry said makes sense. Sometimes we don't know people as well as we think."

"Meaning?"

"Meaning that I'm going to have a talk with Jeremy Tuttle and see what he knows about Deke Walker's love life."

Longarm felt quietly offended by this line of discussion and that he was somehow betraying Deke's friendship. But, on the other hand, if there was even the slightest chance that the late marshal had been interested in Dolly Reardon, then hard questions had to be asked.

"Let's go see Kelly," Longarm decided, tossing his cheroot into the street and heading for the Lumber Mill Saloon.

"I don't think you're in any state of mind to be questioning him."

"I'm a professional," Longarm said, "so let me do the talking, and we'll get along just fine."

William Kelly was almost the exact opposite of Abe Quarry in all respects. He was tall and slender, and it was rumored that he had once been a Mississippi riverboat gambler who had shot no less than five men foolish enough to accuse him of dealing from the bottom of the deck. He wore a mustache and goatee and his manners and dress suggested that he was a dandy.

When Kelly invited them into his plush office and had poured them brandies, he said, "Well, Marshal Long, so you and this handsome young gentleman were sent to find out who murdered Marshal Walker."

"That's right. But after we've caught the killer, Marshal Peacock is staying to take over Walker's place."

Kelly smiled and raised his glass to Rutherford saying, "I wish you well. Reno is a tough town, and there is a real lawless element here that does not take kindly to the law."

"That is of no concern to me," Peacock said. "They'll either abide by the law or else suffer the consequences."

"Strong words for a newly appointed marshal, and one not yet familiar with the West and its ways."

"How did you guess that I'm not from the West?"

"I've lived in New York City and I recognize all the signs," Kelly said. "I think that you must be a very interesting man, and I hope that you are not getting into more of a job than you can safely handle."

"I can take care of myself."

"I'm sure that you can," Kelly said smoothly. "So why are you two here to visit me?"

Longarm leaned forward in his chair. "I guess because

your name was mentioned as someone who had a reason to have Deke Walker murdered."

Kelly chuckled and leaned back farther into his red velvet chair. He sipped at his brandy, then smiled and said, "I liked Deke. He was a good man, and we had an understanding."

"Which was?"

"Deke left me alone, and I left him alone. If I did have a problem, then I took care of it myself. My clientele are rough loggers and mill men. They tend to get rowdy and rambunctious, but they know that I won't put up with fights on the premises."

"If you didn't kill the marshal, who do you think did?"

William Kelly crossed his long legs and smoothed his perfectly tailored pants. "Could have been most anyone."

"Take a guess," Longarm urged.

"All right. I would say that your prime suspect ought to be Miles Reardon. Mr. Reardon is very capable of murder and, from what I've observed and heard, he is obsessed with his daughter and what might happen to his cattle ranch after his death."

"What has Deke Walker's death to do with Mr. Reardon and his daughter?" Peacock asked as innocently as if he'd never heard any of them connected.

"Marshal Walker was courting Miss Reardon!" Kelly laughed and turned his gaze on Longarm. "Or weren't you aware of the fact that you and your late lawman friend were both strongly attracted to the same rich young woman?"

"No," Longarm said. "I wasn't."

"Well, love is blind," Kelly said, as if that explained everything. "And I'm sorry if this news upsets you, but it was obvious to everyone in Reno that Walker was extremely smitten with Miss Reardon. Why, the young woman couldn't come to town without our marshal racing to her side, all smiles and compliments. They always had lunch together, and although I'm not sure if Miss Reardon saw the marshal as a possible suitor, he sure did see her as his future wife."

Peacock glanced at Longarm who was beginning to feel sick to his stomach.

"I am convinced," Kelly continued, "that Marshal Walker had every intention of winning Miss Reardon's heart and hand, then wedding her and becoming part owner in her father's ranch, and someday even taking it over and operating it as he pleased."

"So," Peacock said, "your theory is that Miles Reardon saw through this plan and decided that Walker was unworthy of his daughter and needed to be eliminated?"

"Exactly so! And he, not myself or Abe Quarry or anyone else, should be your prime murder suspect."

"Do you know of anyone who would have been willing to be paid by Miles Reardon to do the job?"

"Of course! The town is full of such low men, if the price was right. And Reardon could certainly afford to pay whatever it took to attract the right killer. But, were I he, I would probably use one of the men on my payroll, rather than someone who lives or works right here in town."

"Why?"

"Why?" Kelly asked rhetorically. "Because then Reardon could better control the killer. Keep him away from any prying authorities like yourselves. Kill him, if necessary, to carry the secret to the grave. Isn't it obvious?"

"No," Longarm said, "it is not."

"Ah, yes," Kelly said. "You are in love with Miss Reardon. And I understand you were a little . . . shall we say, indiscreet . . . along the Truckee River earlier today?"

Longarm could feel his cheeks burning. For crying out loud, this man had already heard about what Arnie and Hannah had witnessed beside the river.

"I wouldn't worry about that," Kelly said. "It isn't the first time that Miss Reardon has been discovered. . . ."

"Stop!" Longarm choked. "Not another word out of your lying mouth or I'll shut it up permanently."

Kelly raised his eyebrows. "Marshal, are you calling me a liar?"

"That's right."

The owner of the Lumber Mill Saloon shook his head. "There was a time, on the Mississippi, that I would have killed you for that foul slander. But I can see that you are being punished enough by the truth concerning your beloved. So I'll just ask you to leave at once."

Longarm came to his feet and then headed out the door. He needed to be alone so that he could think. The idea that Dolly would have had anything to do with Deke, or that she was known for her affairs with men, was something that he was not yet prepared to handle.

"Custis, wait!"

It was Peacock hurrying after him, but Longarm didn't want to talk to the man just now.

"Custis, I'm sorry."

"Get lost! I don't believe either of those lying son of a bitches. They're just trying to throw us off their own trail, can't you see that?"

Peacock overtook him and said, "If Jeremy Tuttle also tells us that Deke Walker was after Miss Reardon, would you finally accept what I suspect is the truth?"

Longarm continued walking. "I guess," he managed to grunt.

"Then come with me to the office, and I'll find the boy

and we'll ask him about Deke and Miss Reardon."

Longarm didn't want to hear any more about them but he knew he had no choice. As painful as the truth might be, it had to be heard and believed.

Chapter 14

When they brought Jeremy into the office the kid was far too excited to sit still. "Have you got something else for me to do?" he asked eagerly.

"As a matter of fact we do," Longarm forced himself to say. "We need some important information."

"On who? Did you talk to Mr. Kelly and Mr. Quarry like I said? What'd they tell you? Bet it was all . . ."

"Jeremy," Longarm said in a stern voice. "Calm down. As you suggested, we talked to both Kelly and Quarry, and it was a good thing that we did."

The would-be lawman beamed. "Bet they told you they had nothing to do with Marshal Walker's ambush. I'll just bet that they both denied everything."

"That's right," Longarm agreed. "As expected. But the question we have right now concerns Marshal Walker."

The kid was caught off guard and his smile faded. He seemed to gather himself as if for an ordeal, then said, "Sure. He and I were *good* friends. We talked all the time."

Longarm looked straight into Jeremy Tuttle's eyes. "You know, after you've been a lawman for a while, you can almost always tell when someone is lying."

"Sure. I can do that already."

"My question is," Longarm said, speaking very slowly, "and I want you to think before you answer and tell me the exact truth."

"Of course I will. I'd never lie to a federal marshal. Gosh, that could get me thrown in prison! Couldn't it?"

"It could," Longarm replied. "False testimony is a crime. So here's the question: Did Marshal Deke Walker show any romantic interest in Miss Dolly Reardon or ever speak to you about winning her hand in marriage?"

Jeremy paled. "I . . . I don't . . ."

"The *truth*," Longarm said, his voice hardening. "It's very important."

"Well," the teenager began, squirming in his chair. "Marshal Walker did think that Miss Reardon was awfully nice and pretty."

"Fine. But did he ever tell you he would like to *marry* her?"

Jeremy's eyes dropped and he looked down at his hands clenched in his lap. "Yeah, he told me that he was in love with her and that he thought that he'd marry her someday."

Longarm expelled an audible breath. "Did the marshal ever tell you anything more about Miss Reardon?"

Jeremy's eyes came up pleading. "Why do you have to know this private stuff?" he asked, sounding miserable.

"We just do," Peacock said quietly. "Did Marshal Walker ever tell you why he wanted to marry Miss Reardon, besides the fact that she was nice and very pretty?"

"He said that he wanted to run her father's big cattle ranch someday. He told me that he could do a better job and that he was getting tired of risking his life for so little pay."

"That's what he said?" Peacock asked.

"Yeah. But he only said it once, when he'd had a few drinks. I never believed he meant it. No, sir. Marshal Walker loved being a lawman and he was the best. Everyone respected him, even if he didn't make much money. He didn't need money, anyway. He slept here half the time and he didn't eat a whole lot. Why would a lawman need much money?"

Longarm could see that Jeremy was troubled. He could only imagine how badly upset the kid had been when Deke had confided his disappointments about being underpaid.

"We all like to get paid what we think we're worth," Longarm told the young man. "And sometimes, a fella gets to thinking that he might like to do something that would make him more money, even if it isn't what he really wants to do."

Jeremy nodded. "Yeah, I guess. The marshal told me that he would like to own some land out in Washoe Valley. He said he'd seen a little ranch down there with a nice house, barn and fences. Marshal Walker said it wasn't a big outfit or anything, but that a man could do just fine on it when he got old. He said he wouldn't mind marrying and having a family some day. Raise some boys . . . like me."

Jeremy almost blushed. "I swear that's exactly what the marshal up and said."

Longarm nodded. "It's a common dream. Most every lawman I know would like to retire someday and have a little spread of his own and a few horses, cows and kids to take care of. Marshal Walker wasn't any different in wanting that than most of us in the profession. But then he said that he was in love with Miss Reardon?"

"Yes sir! And . . . and he knew how you felt about her

151

and that made him feel real bad. I think he worried that he was kind of stabbing you in the back, if you know what I mean."

Longarm knew precisely what the kid was saying. "I never had any hold on Miss Reardon. It wasn't like I owned her or something."

"Exactly," Peacock said with a grin.

Longarm ignored the man and concentrated on Jeremy. "Did Marshal Walker ever talk about Mr. Reardon?"

"In what way?"

"Did he ever say that he knew Mr. Reardon wouldn't be happy about him trying to marry Dolly?"

Jeremy nodded his head. "As a matter of fact he did. The marshal knew that he'd face the same problems with Mr. Reardon that you'd already run up against. That he wasn't good enough or didn't have enough money. Stupid stuff like that."

"I see. Go on."

"I even told the marshal that if he did manage to get hitched to Miss Reardon, he'd prove himself worthy. But I also said I thought he'd be unhappy as a cattle rancher and always having Mr. Reardon watching over his shoulder."

"What did Marshal Walker say to that?" Longarm asked.

"Well," Jeremy answered, "the marshal understood that there'd be problems with old man Reardon. I know that he's run off a lot of his own cowboys that started lookin' too long at Miss Reardon. But Marshal Walker said he wasn't just another broken down cowboy and that he could take care of himself and watch out for his own hide. He said that if Miss Walker ever agreed to marry him, then he'd damn sure handle the old man one way or the other."

"Marshal Walker said that?" Peacock asked, leaning forward with his chin resting on his steepled fingertips.

"Yes, sir! The marshal didn't like Mr. Reardon and I expect that the feeling was mutual."

"Why do you say that?"

"Well," Jeremy said, "they had hard words one time when the marshal rushed over to greet Miss Reardon and then followed her into the merchantile while she shopped. He hadn't seen Mr. Reardon come into town, so when they met, there were bad words."

"Were you there to hear them?"

"I was," Jeremy said. "Mr. Reardon told Marshal Walker to stay the hell away from his daughter . . . or else."

"Or else what?" Longarm asked.

"Or else he'd suffer the consequences of his foolishness."

"That's what Mr. Reardon said?"

"Exactly," the young man replied.

"Then what did Deke . . . I mean Marshal Walker . . . say to that?" Longarm asked.

"Oh, he was real mad. He told that old man that he didn't appreciate being threatened and that he'd visit with Miss Reardon anytime that she came to Reno, so long as she still wanted to visit with him."

"Go on," Peacock said, looking almost excited.

Jeremy shrugged. "So they yelled and cussed at each other a few minutes and then they turned their backs on each other and stomped off madder'n wet hens."

"What did Miss Reardon do?" Peacock asked.

"She just listened. Didn't say a word but I caught her smiling." Jeremy shook his head. "I couldn't figure it out. She looked almost as if . . . as if she was pleased."

Longarm jumped up from his chair and began to pace back and forth in the office. "Jeremy," he asked, "did the marshal and Mr. Reardon ever have hard words again?"

"No, sir. After that, Mr. Reardon didn't come to town very often and, when he did, he left as soon as his business was over. I wasn't the only one that thought they might kill each other out in the street. And I wasn't the only one that noticed that they avoided each other after that day when they got so mad."

"Did Mr. Reardon visit the saloons?"

"Yes, sir."

"Which ones were his favorites?"

"He only had one favorite. It was the Palomino House owned by Mr. Quarry."

Peacock clucked his tongue. "That's very interesting."

"Why is that?" Jeremy asked.

"Because Abe Quarry said that Mr. Reardon ought to be our prime suspect in Deke Walker's murder. You'd think that he'd have more loyalty to a good customer."

Jeremy shrugged his narrow shoulders. "I don't know about that. Sometimes Mr. Reardon, Mr. Quarry and Mr. Kelly would get into all night poker games at the Palomino. I understand that Mr. Reardon would always lose a bunch of money, but he kept coming back."

"Is that a fact?" Longarm asked, surprised that Dolly had never told him about this serious flaw in her father.

"Yes, sir. Once in a while when I was feeding the horses at the stable, I'd see Mr. Reardon leave not long after sunup. He'd be kind of drunk and his foreman would sometimes have to help him into his saddle. Then, they'd ride off and maybe Mr. Reardon wouldn't come back to play poker again for a whole month. But sooner or later, he'd return and then lose his shirt all over again."

Longarm and Peacock exchanged glances and the latter said, "I think this is getting more interesting by the moment. I think we need to ride out first thing tomorrow

154

morning and have a long talk with Miles Reardon. I don't know about you, but I have some tough questions for the man."

"He might refuse to speak to us," Longarm warned.

"What do we do in that case?"

"The only thing we could do is to talk to the judge and get an order to bring him in for questioning. But I doubt Judge Evans would do such a thing."

"I believe he would," Peacock said looking confident. "In fact, I'm sure that he would, if he were asked in the proper way."

"What does that mean?"

"It means that every man . . . even a judge, can be persuaded to do what you want . . . if you find the right incentives."

"Do you think that Judge Evans can be *bought*?"

"I didn't say that."

Longarm frowned. "But that's what you're suggesting."

"Just leave the judge to me if we have to get that order to bring Mr. Reardon in for questioning. I'll handle that problem."

"Fine," Longarm said, suddenly wanting some fresh air. "I'll see you tomorrow morning at eight o'clock down at Fisher's Livery where Jeremy here works when he isn't snooping for us. We'll rent a horse and buggy, and we can be at the Circle R Ranch before noon."

"I'll be ready."

"Can I come along with you?" Jeremy asked. "Please?"

It was against Longarm's better judgment, but the kid had given them so much important information and was so eager that he couldn't resist. "All right."

"Thanks!" Jeremy cried. "And don't worry. I'll just sit quiet as a mouse and not say a word."

"You promise?"

"Yes, sir!"

"All right then," Longarm said, as he headed for the door. "Eight o'clock sharp."

"Custis?"

He turned to look at Peacock. "Yeah?"

"I know this wasn't easy, and it wasn't what you wanted to hear. I'm sorry."

"Don't be," Longarm said. "Nothing has changed about the way I feel toward Miss Reardon. Deke Walker might have disappointed me some, but Dolly never did anything wrong."

"That's not what we heard from Kelly."

"I don't believe the man," Longarm said tightly.

"But you believe Jeremy . . . don't you?"

Longarm glanced at the kid. "Sure. I believe him."

"Marshal Long?" Jeremy said, his voice sounding hollow. "There's just one other thing that I didn't tell you. I don't want to make you angry or anything but . . ."

Longarm didn't think he wanted to hear any more but he had no choice. "What is it?"

"I seen Miss Reardon *kissing* the marshal. I seen her and him go up to a hotel room . . . bunches of times."

Longarm could feel his face tighten so hard that it felt as if it were made of dried mud cracking under the burning rays of the sun. "You sure of that?"

"I'm sorry, but yes, sir."

"Well," Longarm managed to say. "Why don't we just keep that bit of information to ourselves."

"Yes, sir. You love her, don't you?"

"I do," Longarm said a moment before he turned to leave and go off to find a bottle of whiskey and a private place to get drunk.

"Or at least . . . I did."

Chapter 15

Longarm was not in the best of moods the next morning when he dragged his hangover and carcass over to the livery shortly after eight o'clock. He'd neglected to shave and his eyeballs were bloodshot.

"Looks like you had quite an evening," Peacock said. "You aren't going to throw up on us in the buggy, are you?"

"I'll be fine. Just need some fresh air. A long drive in the country will do me wonders."

"I sure hope so. Jeremy is getting the rig hitched up out behind the barn. We ought to be able to leave in about fifteen minutes."

"Fine," Longarm said. "Stop by the cafe where we had breakfast and pick me up on your way out. I need some coffee."

"Maybe you should just stay here and let . . ."

"Not a chance," Longarm told the man as he turned and trudged off toward the cafe.

Longarm was able to down two cups of strong black coffee before Jeremy drove a buckboard up in front of the cafe. Longarm dropped a dollar on the counter and said to the owner, "You don't have any headache powders for sale, do you?"

"Sure. We sell lots of that stuff, and you look like you could use a double dose. You want it with water or coffee?"

"One more cup of strong coffee along with your headache powders will put me in fine fettle."

"Don't know about that, but you look like you're going to make it after all," the cafe owner said. "Marshal, when you first staggered in here, I thought you might be on your last legs."

Longarm felt insulted. "Mister, I've been shot, stabbed, stomped and damn near scalped, so a little hangover isn't a big problem."

"Glad to hear that, Marshal. The word is that you and Miss Reardon had quite a time yesterday afternoon along the banks of the Truckee. Lucky bastard."

Longarm didn't say a word. Instead, he emptied the powders into his third cup of coffee and downed it in three gulps. Then, he headed out to the street and climbed into the buckboard beside Peacock.

"You're looking slightly more alive than before," the marshal said.

"Let's just dispense with the chatter. All right? And anyway, I thought we were using a buggy, not a damned buckboard."

"Sorry," Jeremy said. "The buggy was broke, and this was all I could get to use."

"Fine," Longarm said, knowing he was going to pay because a buckboard was a hard riding vehicle and it would give his head fits.

"All right, Jeremy," Peacock said, "drive us out to the Circle R and don't spare these horses."

"Yes, sir!"

• • •

Despite the bad road and hard jolts he'd taken in the buck-board, by eleven-thirty Longarm was feeling halfway decent, although he was still filled with anger and sadness about Dolly. She had lied to him when she said that she hadn't been with any other men during their most recent separation. And, if she'd lied about that, she was capable of lying about most anything else.

No doubt about it, Longarm decided, *I am done with her*. And although he felt hurt by her deception, in a way he was also relieved that he would not be getting married and complicating his life. Once a man got married, he was no longer the captain of his own ship, the master of his own destiny. Suddenly, every decision had to be made in tandem with his wife and then later with kids in mind.

Longarm had enjoyed his freedom too long to give it up without regrets, and now he wouldn't have to face inevitability.

"So how are we going to handle this?" Rutherford asked when they saw the sign notifying them that they were about to pass onto the Circle R Ranch.

"Handle what?" Longarm asked. "The fact that the woman I loved lied to me and had an affair with my friend . . . or the fact that her father might have had my friend killed?"

"Both."

"I just don't think there's any way to plan this out," Longarm replied. "If both Dolly and her father are home and come out to greet us, I'll speak to Miles Reardon first and then take Dolly aside and tell her what I've learned from Jeremy."

"Oh, please don't do that!" Jeremy protested. "I don't want to get into any trouble. Mr. Reardon could get me fired . . . or a lot worse."

159

"He's right," Peacock added. "What Jeremy told us yesterday is no doubt common knowledge in Reno. It serves no purpose to mention our source of information, and it could put Jeremy in a dangerous spot."

"I agree," Longarm said. "We'll just state our case and let the cards fall where they may."

"Thanks," Jeremy said with obvious relief.

They saw the main ranch house, barns, corrals and outbuildings when they topped a low rise of land and Peacock shook his head with admiration. "Why, the Circle R is as pretty as a picture. How many acres do you think they own?"

"I don't know," Longarm said. "Jeremy?"

"At least five thousand," the kid told them. "Mr. Reardon's father was one of the first cattlemen in this part of Nevada and he grabbed the best land and water. The cowboys I've talked to that work for the Circle R say it's the finest ranch for a hundred miles in any direction."

"I can easily believe that," Peacock said, obviously impressed by what could be seen of the lush valley and ranch headquarters.

"Just be on your guard for whatever may happen," Longarm warned. "Reardon is unpredictable and I've heard, the older he gets, the more cunning and cantankerous he's become."

Jeremy nodded. "I've heard stories of him taking a bullwhip to cowboys who don't do what they've been told. If you don't mind, I think I'll kind of stay behind with the buggy just in case you get Mr. Reardon mad and bullets start flying."

"That would be fine," Longarm said. "Are you armed?"

"You mean am I packing a hideout gun in my coat pocket?" Jeremy patted his coat. "You bet I am! I don't trust that ornery old man any further than I could throw him."

"All right then," Longarm said. "We just ride in and speak our piece to Reardon and see what he has to say in return."

Peacock nodded. "I guess that's all that we can do. I did talk to Judge Evans last evening, and he agreed to give us a court summons for Mr. Reardon should he refuse to cooperate."

That surprised Longarm. "Nice work!"

"I can tell you that the judge's cooperation didn't come easy or cheap."

Longarm took that to mean that Peacock had paid the judge money, but he didn't want to know for sure, so he said nothing as they approached the ranch yard.

The Reardon house was a sprawling, two-story Victorian. It seemed out of place sitting in the West instead of in Charleston or somewhere else in the Old South. It boasted stately columns and a wide veranda fronted by roses and vines. There were rocking chairs on the porch and even a porch swing which Longarm had once briefly enjoyed while kissing Dolly on a moonlit evening. But that was all in the past. Now, he reminded himself, they were here on business that was going to be more than merely unpleasant.

As Jeremy drove into the ranch yard, Reardon and Dolly, along with several of their house servants, appeared on the veranda. When the old man recognized Longarm, he said something to Dolly, but she shook her head and Longarm had the impression that she had refused to go back into the house.

"What do you want?" Reardon demanded as he stood with his feet wide apart and his hands on his hips. "Marshal Long, you know that you've been warned never to trespass on my property!"

Longarm had prepared himself for the worst kind of confrontation, so the old man's shouting neither surprised nor upset him. "Rein 'em in, Jeremy."

When the buckboard came to a halt, Dolly raced past her father taking the stairs two at a time. She threw herself at Longarm and hugged him around the waist. "You shouldn't have come like this," she whispered. "You should have waited like we agreed."

Longarm pushed her away. "I came to talk to your father about Deke Walker, not about us. Why don't you go inside."

She looked up at him. "What's wrong?"

Longarm didn't want to discuss her lies in front of anyone, so he said, "Dolly, we can talk about us later."

"No!" she cried. "What is the matter? I have to know."

"Dolly," her father roared, "quit humiliating both of us and go inside right now!"

"Father, Custis and I are getting married!"

"The hell you are!" her father bellowed.

"No, we're not," Longarm said in a low, firm voice.

Dolly's face went slack with shock. "Custis, what are you doing to us?"

"Saying good-bye," he replied. "You and Deke had an affair. I could have forgiven that, given that I didn't swear off the opposite sex, either. But I told you the truth, and you lied to me. I can't abide a liar, Dolly. It's over between us."

She took a step back and her eyes hardened. "Over? It's over when I say it's over. Who do you think you are to tell me that we're through? You're a nobody, Custis. Just a man with a big gun."

162

"Why didn't you tell me that your father vowed to kill Deke if he kept after you?"

"Because it was none of your damned business!"

Peacock cleared his voice and said, "I beg to differ with that statement, Miss Reardon. We're officers of the law investigating the murder of a federal officer. Because your father and Marshal Walker had words over you, I'm afraid that he's now a prime suspect."

Dolly turned to Peacock and studied him for a moment. "Marshal," she said, "I can't forgive Custis for just making a fool out of himself, but at least you have the excuse of being new to the West and your job. So I'll tell you right now not to push this any further. What all three of you need to do is to get back in the buggy and just go away."

"Can't do that," Peacock replied. "I'm sorry, but we have to talk to your father about Deke Walker."

Reardon came off the veranda and Longarm saw the old man's hand go for the gun he wore on his hip. There was no doubt that the fool was crazy enough to shoot him, Peacock, and just for good measure, Jeremy Tuttle. And so Longarm lunged at Reardon and just managed to slam his fist down on the rancher's forearm, knocking the Colt revolver to the ground. Then, Longarm grabbed Reardon by the front of his coat and hurled him to the ground.

"Stop that!" Dolly cried, attacking Longarm with her clenched fists.

"Get her away from me!" Longarm shouted.

Peacock grabbed Dolly and pulled her away kicking and screaming. A pair of cowboys burst out of the barn and came running with pitchforks. Longarm drew his own gun and pointed it in their direction yelling, "Get back to work! We're taking the old man into town on the orders of Judge Evans."

The cowboys skidded to a halt, pitchforks raised and looking as if they might be foolish enough to attack a man with a loaded gun. Thankfully, they had a moment of clarity and backed away. One of them shouted, "Mr. Reardon, what do you want us to do?"

"Kill them all!"

Longarm didn't have a pair of handcuffs, but he did have a big advantage in both his size and his strength, so he picked Reardon up and tossed him into the back of the buckboard.

"Let's go before this gets any worse!" he shouted.

Jeremy didn't need any convincing. He jumped back into the driver's seat and was turning the rig around when Peacock joined them on the run.

"I'll kill all of you! I'll have you hanged!" Reardon was screaming over and over.

"Can he do that?" Jeremy asked looking badly shaken as he forced their team of horses into a hard run.

"No," Longarm snarled, sitting on the old man to keep him under control. "As long as we have that order from Judge Evans, we can bring him in and throw him in jail until he's ready to truthfully answer our questions."

"Actually," Rutherford yelled over the shouting and the pounding of hoofbeats and the jolting of the buggy, "Judge Evans didn't exactly give me *complete* authority to do this."

Longarm couldn't believe his ears. "What?"

"He said that he'd probably give us a warrant if it actually became necessary to take Mr. Reardon in by force."

"Well, it *was* necessary."

"Exactly," Peacock said, hanging onto the buggy and staring straight ahead as they shot up the road that would take them back to Reno.

Chapter 16

Miles Reardon did not stop yelling and raising Cain until they had searched him and locked him up in the lone jail cell. By then, the old man's throat was so hoarse that his voice was gone, but he was still spitting and fighting.

"I've never seen anyone so mad," Peacock said, looking shaken and anxious as they stepped outside to talk. "He's a maniac."

"A *rich* maniac," Longarm added. "And no doubt one who has every intention of nailing our hides to the wall. We'll hold him overnight and then start on him first thing in the morning. He couldn't tell us anything now even if he wanted to."

"I'd probably better go see Judge Evans again. Poor Jeremy Tuttle is really shook up. He's worried sick about Reardon getting him fired or killed."

"I'm a little worried about that myself. The old man has gone completely off his rocker."

Peacock nodded. "It's easy to see that he is violent and no doubt either killed Marshal Walker or had him killed."

"Yep," Longarm agreed. "Are you going to stay here at the jail all night?"

"I sure wasn't counting on it."

"Then count again," Longarm said. "Did you notice all the people that came out onto the boardwalk when we brought Reardon into town? This has caused quite a stir, and you can bet we've uncovered a hornet's nest. Even a man crazy as Reardon is bound to have his supporters, given the amount of business that he offers Reno. Unless I'm badly mistaken, you can expect to see the mayor, the city council and even Judge Evans before long."

"What am I going to tell them? That Jeremy Tuttle overheard Reardon and Marshal Walker in a bad argument? That's not going to be convincing enough to satisfy anyone."

Longarm frowned. "You're right. We've got to get the old man to confess, and we've got to do it quickly. I know Judge Evans, and while you might have greased his palms, he's not one to go against the tide of popular opinion. He'll buckle under the pressure."

"So what are we supposed to do? If that man gets set free, we'll never get him back in jail or be able to get a confession."

"You're right."

"Well, then?"

Longarm was tired and hungry. He scratched the stubble on his face and said, "I don't know the answer to that question, Marshal Peacock. When we left this morning, you led me to believe that Judge Evans was in our corner. Now, you're telling me he really isn't."

"Would you have gone out to see Reardon if I hadn't led you to believe the judge was on our side?"

"Yes."

"And could we have done anything different given that the man went for his gun with every intention of killing all three of us?"

"No."

"Then, what else could we have done?"

"Not much," Longarm admitted. "That old man wasn't about to cooperate."

"Then what can we do?"

"Well," Longarm said, "I'm going to go have something to eat and I'm dog-tired. I'm going to take a bath and go to bed. Good night, Marshal."

"Wait a damn minute!" Peacock cried. "You can't do this to me! We're in this mess together."

"Nope," Longarm decided. "I'm not the marshal in charge here and that isn't my jail, it's yours. So just do your best and try to get someone to bring you food. I expect Reardon will settle down after dark, and you can both get some sleep."

"But you said the mayor and the town council and . . ."

"I was only guessing," Longarm told him a moment before he turned and walked away.

Two hours later, Longarm was feeling a whole lot better. He'd shaved, had a good steak dinner and a beer and now he was resting in a bathtub filled with hot, soapy water. He had decided that he was lucky that he'd found out the truth about Dolly Reardon, and he remembered how hard and vicious she'd become when she realized that he wasn't going to go forward with their plans to get married. Right then, he'd seen her true nature and he couldn't understand how he could have been so blind. Probably because he and Dolly made exceptional love. That could and often did ruin a man's normally good judgment.

The only thing that Longarm didn't feel good about was what might well happen to Rutherford or even Jeremy. Longarm had no doubt that the old man would exact vengeance once he was released from jail. And although he might be guilty of killing Deke Walker, he'd probably get off scot-free. That was the part that really upset Longarm. It meant that the work of finding Walker's killer wasn't completed and that he'd have to stay in Reno and keep working. It also meant that he'd have to somehow protect Peacock and the kid, which would be no easy task.

"Marshal!"

Longarm's eyes were almost closed and he was smoking a cigar in the bathtub when he heard his name called.

"Marshal Long!"

"What now?" he groaned.

The hotel clerk burst into the room. "There's been a shoot-out at the marshal's office!"

Longarm's jaw dropped, his cheroot fell forgotten into the water, sizzled and sank. "Was anyone killed?"

"I don't know. There's a big crowd gathered at the door. Didn't you hear all the shots?"

"No. I was splashing around too much."

"Well, there was about four shots. You better get over there fast."

"Yeah," Longarm muttered as he crawled out of the bathtub and grabbed his clothes without even bothering to use a towel. In his haste, he slipped on the wet floor while trying to pull on his boots and fell hard. Swearing and fuming, he managed to get the boots on over his sopping wet stockings then lunged for his hat and gunbelt.

When he burst out the front door of the hotel, he collided with someone and bowled them over. It was dark outside now and as Longarm ran up Virginia Street and across the bridge at the Truckee, he could see a big crowd gathered in front of the marshal's office.

"Move aside!" he yelled breathlessly as he slammed through the crowd and charged into the office to see it filled with people. "Move aside!"

The first man he saw was Rutherford Peacock lying on the floor in a pool of blood. Longarm pushed a gawking man aside and knelt by the Easterner, who he could see was still breathing, although he was in bad shape.

"Custis," Peacock whispered. "Someone must have slipped Reardon a gun through the window when I stepped outside for a moment to talk to the mayor. When I came back in, the old man opened fire on me. Did I get him?"

"I don't know." Longarm turned to someone and asked, "Did the marshal get Reardon?"

"Yep, plugged him right through the gizzard. By gawd, the marshal shot Mr. Reardon dead!"

"Someone find a doctor!" Longarm yelled.

"There's already one on the way."

Rutherford was pale and frightened. "Custis, I'm not ready to die so young."

Longarm pulled Rutherford's coat open and then tore his shirt until he could inspect the wound. It was in the chest, but it might have missed his lungs because it was low and several inches to the right of Peacock's heart.

"Am I dying?" Rutherford whispered. "Just tell me the truth. I don't want to die but . . ."

"Shut up and rest easy," Longarm instructed. "I'm going to roll you over just a little, and it will hurt, but I have to see if the bullet went through your back or if it's still buried inside your rib cage."

"I couldn't believe it when Reardon opened fire. I think a couple of his bullets as well as mine struck the bars. Bullets were ricocheting all over the damn place and . . ."

Longarm rolled him sideways and saw that the bullet had passed completely through the man's body. "Good news. The doc isn't going to have to mine you for lead."

"I feel real light-headed and dizzy. Am I going to die? I have some family and . . ."

"Listen," Longarm said with exasperation, "you aren't going to die, but you're about to talk *me* plumb to death!"

Peacock actually smiled. "You're as hard as an anvil, Custis Long, but I'm glad you're here to take charge because . . ."

Peacock stiffened and suddenly lost consciousness.

"Is he dead?" someone asked, leaning over Longarm and staring, just inches from Peacock's face.

"No. Now get back!"

"But I'm the damned doctor."

Longarm twisted around to see a bespectacled man in his sixties with rumpled gray hair and foul smelling breath. "*You're* the doctor?"

"That's right. Were you expecting someone else? If so, then I'll go back to my poker game."

"Just get to work and stop the bleeding. The bullet passed through his body."

The doctor wasn't very professional or clean. He was probably just a man who had learned to save lives during The War Between the States or else had studied briefly under a real doctor and took a short correspondence course. However, he did know how to bandage a wound expertly enough to stop the bleeding. Once that was accomplished, he gave the order that Peacock was to be laid out on the two office desks and covered with blankets.

"That's all you can do?" Longarm fretted.

"I got the bleeding under control. Now, it's just a matter of time until we see if he's gone into shock and dies . . . or if he's young and strong enough to pull through."

Longarm could see that this made sense. He turned to the crowded room and yelled, "Everyone outside right now!"

There was a lot of grumbling, but Longarm was in no mood for arguments and soon had the room cleared except for the doctor, Judge Evans and a man who quickly introduced himself as Mayor Maury Watson.

"What happened here?" the judge asked.

Longarm glanced over at Peacock. "Someone slipped Miles Reardon a gun through the back window and the old fool opened fire on your new marshal. Rutherford said that he returned fire and was lucky enough to put Reardon down for keeps."

The judge went over to the jail cell, which was still locked. Even so, he tried to push the door open and, when he failed, he said, "Marshal Long, do you know where we can find the keys to this cell?"

"They're in one of these desk drawers."

It only took a moment to find the keys and then open the cell. Both the men went inside and Longarm heard the doctor say, "Three bullets in him. He was probably shot dead on his feet."

"Miles Reardon was a crazy old fool," the judge said. "But I always got along well enough with him. Maybe that was because we never had any issues between us. I did know that I never wanted to be his enemy."

Longarm left Peacock for a moment and went to examine the rancher's body. It had happened as described, and Reardon's body was a riddled mess. One of the shots had struck him right between the eyes and blown out the back of his skull.

"What are we going to do about this?" the mayor asked. "We've just lost our new marshal and the richest man in the county."

"I'll demand an inquiry," Evans said after a long pause. "Obviously, we'd like to know who passed Miles Reardon

171

a gun through the cell window, but I doubt that will be possible."

Longarm saw a kerosene lamp hanging on a peg. He lit it and headed outside and around to the back alley. Several people followed him, but none of them were stupid enough to ask questions. When he knelt by the window, Longarm studied the footprints. They were unusual in that they were small. Too small for a man.

"Mean anything to you?" someone finally asked.

Longarm ignored the question. He knew who had been outside the window, because there was only one person who would have had the courage and the motive to do such a terrible and deadly thing.

Miss Dolly Reardon.

Longarm hurried back into the office. He cornered the doctor and said, "I'll expect you to stay here with Marshal Peacock as long as it takes to pull him through."

"Sure. But I don't work for drinks or small change. No, sir! My fee for staying up all night and saving this man's life will be one hundred dollars. Take it . . . or I leave him and go back to the poker table."

"What kind of a damn doctor are you?" Longarm shouted, jerking the man up on his toes.

"I'm a doctor who is a hundred dollars in debt to the dealer. Now, do we have an understanding, or not?"

Longarm released the sorry excuse for a doctor and said, "All right. If Marshal Peacock lives, you get the hundred dollars. But, if he doesn't live, you'll need your own services. Understood?"

The man nodded and swallowed hard.

Longarm turned on his heel and headed for the door. The shooting hadn't happened more than thirty minutes earlier and, if he knew Dolly, she was on her lonely way back to the Circle R Ranch. If he could catch her on the road before she had the protection of her cowboys, then he might well be able to get a confession.

If not . . . well, he'd get one anyhow.

Chapter 17

It was well after midnight when Longarm finally rode a hastily borrowed horse into the Circle R Ranch yard. They must have heard the drum of his horse's hoofbeats, because Dolly was standing on the porch and so were her cowboys, most of them still in long underwear, but all of them armed and ready to fight.

Longarm was exhausted, but he managed a thin smile in the lamplight and his eyes settled on Dolly, who looked just as weary as himself. "Good evening," he said to her.

"What do you want? What have you done with my father?"

Longarm hadn't seen any hoofprints on the road from Reno, but he was sure that Dolly must have cut across country on some shortcut that only she and her cowboys would know. He looked around at the grim-faced cowboys and knew that he was in a bad position.

"Dolly," he said, twisting back in the saddle and facing her, "we need to talk."

"About what?" she demanded. "I think you said everything you had to say earlier. I know I've nothing left to say to you."

"I only wish that were the case."

Spider McGee detached from the other cowboys. He had his pants on, but no shirt. There was a six-gun in his hand, but it was hanging by his side and, when he spoke, his voice was very soft. "Marshal, are you calling Miss Reardon a liar?"

"I'm saying that I think she knows more about her father than she is admitting."

McGee didn't quite know how to react and before he could decide what to do, Dolly said, "State your business, Custis."

"I want you to come into town with me."

"Why?"

"We need to talk about your father."

"You let him go free, and I'll come into town. Otherwise, no deal."

Longarm could see that this was going to go down the hard way. "Dolly," he said, "you know that your father can't do that."

"He can if you let him."

"Uh-uh," Longarm said. "Thanks to you slipping him a gun from the back alley through his cell bars this evening, he shot and almost killed Marshal Peacock."

Even in the poor lamplight, he saw her start and then bring her hand up to her mouth. "What are you talking about?"

"You slipped your father a gun, and he shot it out with the marshal. Both of them were hit, and your father was killed."

"Oh, no!" she cried.

Longarm saw her crumple at the knees, and before he could get off his horse, Spider and several other cowboys had her supported and were leading her to one of the rocking chairs.

"Marshal, what the hell are you talking about?" McGee shouted, his gun now up and pointed at Longarm. "Miss Reardon ain't gone anywhere today."

"That's not true," Longarm said. "You're just lying to protect her. She rode to Reno and thought she could help her father by getting him a loaded Colt. Unfortunately, he got himself killed instead."

"The hell you say!" McGee shouted. "We've all been here with her all day talking about what to do about Mr. Reardon. We almost came into town to free him from the jail, but Miss Reardon said that we should give it a day before we acted."

Now, it was Longarm's turn to be stunned. He twisted around looking at all the cowboys and even the housekeepers. "Are all of you people going to stand by that story?"

To a person, they nodded. A Mexican housekeeper in her sixties said in broken English, "Miss Reardon, she no go nowhere, senor! This I swear on my mother's and Jesus' grave."

Longarm inhaled deeply, as if a strong breath of fresh night air could clear his weary mind. It just didn't seem possible that he could be wrong. Who else with such small feet could have slipped Miles Reardon a gun if not his daughter?

And then it hit him. Hit him so hard he almost toppled from his saddle.

Little Jeremy Tuttle. He had feet no bigger than that of a woman.

"Marshal," McGee said, "I think maybe you'd better clear out of here pronto, before we decide to let you know what we think of you for arresting Mr. Reardon. I think you'd better ride out of here fast."

"No," Dolly said, coming out of her chair. "At least, not until I make a confession."

Longarm couldn't stay upright in his saddle anymore. On legs that were almost rubbery, he climbed off his horse and then tramped up on the porch and took a chair. The cowboys crowded around and Longarm removed his hat and cradled his head in his hands.

"Custis."

He raised his head. "Yeah?"

"I owe you the truth."

"I guess you do."

"I didn't go anywhere today, so I really don't know who slipped a gun to my father. You have to believe that."

Longarm sighed. He studied all the faces ringed around him. "I believe you, Dolly. You lied to me about some important things, but this isn't one of them."

"Then who did give my father a gun?"

He pushed himself to his feet. "I can't say."

"You mean you *won't* say."

"That's right, because I don't know for certain."

Dolly thought about that for a moment. "As long as my father is dead, I might as well tell you that he never killed Marshal Walker. There was a man named Harley."

"Harley?"

"Yes. No last name. He just called himself Harley. I didn't know him, and neither did the other men that work for us. He showed up here at the ranch one day, and he didn't stay long. But I could tell he wasn't a cowboy looking for ranch work. It was obvious that Harley was a professional gunman."

Longarm was suddenly wide awake. "So did your father pay this man Harley to kill Marshal Walker?"

Dolly was slow to answer, but finally whispered, "Yes."

"Give me a description and tell me everything you

178

know about the man." Longarm started for his horse. "I'll find him no matter how long it takes."

"You don't have to do that."

"What do you mean?" Longarm asked, turning on the steps.

"Harley is dead."

"Dead?"

"That's right. On the night that Marshal Walker was murdered, Harley returned and started bragging about the job he did and then he demanded a whole lot of money." Dolly shook her head. "Father carried a hideout gun in his boot. He shot Harley to death in his library. We buried that killer out in our cemetery. You can dig him up if you think I'm lying, but he's going to be badly decomposed. I expect that Harley would be just bones by now."

Longarm rubbed his burning eyeballs. "Dammit, Dolly, are you sure this is the truth? I'm so tired of hearing lies."

"As God is my witness, it's the truth," the Mexican housekeeper swore, making the sign of the cross. "This Harley, he was a very evil hombre. *El Diablo*."

"It's the truth," Spider McGee seconded. "We heard Mr. Reardon and Harley shouting, and then there was a single gunshot. We rushed to the house and the stranger was dead. We just didn't know why or what had gone on here. It wasn't right that Mr. Reardon paid him to kill Marshal Walker. But it ain't right of you to accuse Miss Reardon of leaving this ranch today and slipping her father a gun 'cause it damn sure didn't happen."

"All right," Longarm said, convinced that he had, at last, learned the truth. "It's over."

"Not until I know who slipped my father a gun that got him killed," Dolly said through clenched teeth.

"Look," Longarm said, trying his level best not to lose his temper. "Your father was every bit as guilty of killing my friend . . . *and your lover* . . . Marshall Walker, as this Harley fella. Mr. Reardon would have gone to prison for the rest of his life if the truth came out and he stood trial for his crime. Do you really think your father would have wanted to have a lifelong prison sentence?"

Dolly said nothing.

"I don't," Spider said. "Mr. Reardon couldn't have stood to be in prison."

"Of course he couldn't have," Longarm said. "So, in a way, whoever gave him the gun did him a favor, although he nearly got Marshal Peacock killed. What I'm saying is that this pathetic mess of murder and lies ends here. Right now. Tonight. No more!"

Longarm's voice was raw and shaking with anger. "Can we agree on that?"

Dolly dipped her chin in agreement. "All right. It's over."

"Do I have your word?" He searched their faces. "Do I have everyone here's word that this murdering business is finished?"

They all nodded. Dolly. McGee. Even the Mexican woman who kept crossing herself and every Circle R cowboy.

"Then, it is *finished*!" Longarm said as he went back and mounted his horse.

"Custis!"

He turned at the sound of her voice. "Yes?"

"You're out on your feet. You can sleep in our bunkhouse. There's an extra bed."

"No, thanks," he said. "I've seen about as much of you and this ranch as I care to see in one lifetime."

And having said that and they having given their word that it was finished, Longarm rode out of the lamplight and back into the darkness.

Chapter 18

It took Longarm three days but he finally found Jeremy Tuttle. The young man was half drunk in the Bucket of Blood Saloon up in Virginia City.

"Hello, kid."

"Marshal Long!"

"Took me a while to find you," Longarm said, taking a seat at Jeremy's table. "I don't like wasting my time."

"I'm a big waste of time all right," the kid replied. "Nothing but a damn waste of time and space. I should never have been born. Now, I'm going to get hanged."

"For slipping that gun to Mr. Reardon."

"Yeah, for giving him the gun he used to kill Marshal Peacock."

"He didn't quite do the job," Longarm said. "Rutherford is going to make it."

Jeremy looked stunned. "But I saw him go down with a bullet in the chest. Saw it through the window bars!"

"Not the heart, Jeremy. And not the lungs. Rutherford got lucky and he's going to make it."

Tears rolled down the kid's cheeks. "Oh, I'm so glad! He's kind of . . . well, different. But Marshal Peacock is a good man. I sure didn't want him to get killed."

"You made a bad mistake that night. Did you think that Reardon was just going to scare Rutherford with a loaded gun?"

"He told me he wouldn't need to use it. He said that he'd just get the drop on the marshal and that all he wanted to do was to go free."

"You shouldn't have believed him."

"He also said that if I didn't help him, he'd have me killed. Mr. Reardon swore he'd do that."

"When?"

"We were alone for a minute after we got him back to Reno. That's when he told me I was either going to help him get a gun or I was as good as dead. Marshal Long, you just have to believe me!"

"I do," Longarm said. "Lately, I'm having to believe everyone."

"But even so, I was a low coward," Jeremy breathed, reaching for the whiskey bottle. "I was just scared and trying to save myself."

Longarm took the bottle away. "We're going back to Reno and you're going to apologize and tell Marshal Peacock the same thing you just told me."

"Oh, please. No!"

"You got to do it," Longarm ordered. "You owe it to Rutherford and you owe it to yourself to confess your mistake and ask for his forgiveness. Otherwise, this is going to eat you up and you'll never be worth a damn."

Jeremy nodded. "All right. I'll do it. Then you'll send me to prison?"

"No," Longarm said. "Then the slate is wiped clean and you leave Reno and promise me that you'll do something with your life. Something good."

Jeremy dipped his chin. "I promise. But I know that I

ain't got what it takes to become a federal marshal. I'll never be man enough to be a federal marshal."

Longarm laid his hand on the kid's shoulder. "I think you might be wrong."

"Really?" Jeremy grinned.

"Really," Longarm said, getting out of his chair and helping the kid to his feet. "Now, let's get out of here."

"If Marshal Peacock doesn't want to whip me senseless or kill me, maybe I could go to Denver with you," Jeremy dared to suggest. "Maybe you could show me the town and . . . and how to be man enough to wear a *star!*"

Longarm had to grin. "Maybe I can," he agreed, helping steer the kid out of the Bucket of Blood Saloon.

Watch for

Longarm and the Lady Hustlers

292nd novel in the exciting LONGARM series
from Jove

Coming in March!

LONGARM

Explore the exciting Old West with one of the men who made it wild!